THE BEGONIA KILLER

JEFF BOND

ISBN: 978-1-7346225-2-2

www.thirdchancestories.com

For my mother.

CHAPTER ONE

After twenty minutes on Martha Dodson's couch, listening to her suspicions about the neighbor, I respected the woman. She was no idle snoop. She'd noticed his compulsive begonia care out the window while making lavender sachets from burlap scraps. She hadn't even been aware of the papered-over bedroom above his garage until her postal carrier had commented.

I asked, "And the day he removed the begonias, how did you happen to see that?"

Martha set tea before me on a coaster, twisting the cup so its handle faced me. "Ziggy and I were out for a walk—he'd just done his business. I stood up to knot the bag..." Her kindly face curdled, and I thought she might be remembering the product of Ziggy's "business" until she finished, "Then we saw him start *hacking*, and scowling, and *thrusting* those clippers at his flowers."

Her eyes, a pleasing hazel shade, darkened at the memory.

She added, "At his own flowers."

I shifted my skirt, giving her a moment. "The begonias were in a mailbox planter?"

"Right by the street, yes. The whole incident happened just a few feet from passing cars, from the sidewalk where parents push babies in strollers."

"Did he dispose of the mess afterward?"

"Immediately," Martha said. "He looked at his clippers for a second—the blades were streaked with green from all those leaves and stems he'd destroyed—then he sort of recovered. He picked everything up and placed it in the yard-waste bin. Every last petal."

"He sounds meticulous."

"Extremely."

I jotted *Cleaned up begonia mess* in my notebook.

Maybe because of my psychology background—I'm twelve credit hours shy of a PhD—I like to start these introductory interviews by allowing clients time to just talk, open-ended. I want to know what *they* feel is important. Often, this tells as much about them as it does about whatever they're asking me to investigate.

Martha Dodson had talked about children first. Hers were in college. *Did I have little ones?* I'd waived my usual practice of withholding personal information and said yes, six and fourteen. She'd clapped and rubbed her hands. *Wonderful! Where did they go to school?*

Next, we'd talked crafting. Martha liked to knit and make felt flowers for centerpieces, for vase arrangements, even to decorate shoes—that type of crafter whose creativity spills beyond the available mediums and fills a house, infusing every shelf and surface.

Only with this groundwork lain had she told me about

the case itself, describing the various oddities of her neighbor three doors down, Kent Kirkland.

I was still waiting to hear the crux of her problem, the reason she wanted to hire McGill Investigators. (Full disclosure—although the name is plural, there's only one investigator: Molly McGill. Me.)

"That sounds like an intense, visceral moment," I said, squaring myself to Martha on the couch. "So has he done something to your flowers? Are you engaged in a dispute with him?"

Martha shook her head. Then, with perfect composure, she said, "I think he's keeping a boy in the bedroom over his garage."

I felt like somebody had blasted jets of freezing air into both my ears. The pen I'd been taking notes with tumbled from my hand to the carpet.

"Wait, *keeping* a boy?" I said.

"Yes."

"Against his will? As in, kidnapping?"

Martha nodded.

I was having trouble reconciling this woman in front of me—cardigan sweater, hair in a layered bob—with the accusation she'd just uttered. We were sitting in a nice New Jersey neighborhood. Nicer than mine. We were drinking tea.

She said, "There might be two."

Now my notebook dropped to the carpet.

"Two?" I said. "You think this man is holding two boys hostage?"

"I don't know for sure," she said. "If I knew for sure, I'd be over there breaking down the door myself. But I suspect it."

She explained that a ten-year-old boy from the next town over had gone missing six months ago. The parents had been quoted as saying they "lost track of" their son. They hadn't reported his disappearance until the evening after they'd last seen him.

"The mother told reporters he wanted a scooter for Christmas, one of those cute kick scooters." Martha sniffled at the memory. "Guess what I saw the UPS driver drop off on Kent Kirkland's porch two weeks ago?"

"A scooter," I said.

Her eyes flashed. "A very large box from a company that makes scooters."

Having retrieved my notebook, I jotted, *box delivery (scooter?)*. We talked a bit about this scooter company—which also made bikes, dehumidifiers, and air fryers.

Scooter or not, there remained about a million dots to be connected from this boy's case, which I vaguely remembered from news reports, to Kent Kirkland.

I left the dots aside for now. "How do you get to two boys?"

"There was another missing boy, about the same age. During the summer." Martha's mouth moved in place like she was counting up how many jars of tomatoes she'd canned yesterday. "He lived close too. That case was complicated because the parents had just divorced, and the dad—who was a native Venezuelan—had just moved back. People suspected him of taking the boy with him."

"To Venezuela?"

"Yes. Apparently the State Department couldn't get any answers."

I nodded, not because I accepted all that she was telling

me, but because there was no other polite response available.

Neither of us spoke. Our eyes drifted together down the street to Kent Kirkland's two-story saltbox home. Pale-yellow vinyl siding. Tall privacy fence. Three separate posted notices to *Please pick up after your pet*. Neighborhood Watch sign at the corner.

Finally, I said, "Look, Mrs. Dodson. Martha. Most of the cases we handle at McGill Investigators are domestic in nature. Straying husbands. Teenagers mixed up with the wrong crowd. I'm a mother myself, and I've been a wife. Twice." I softened this disclosure with a smirk. "I generally take cases where my own life experiences can be brought to bear."

"But that's why I chose you." Martha worried her hands in her lap. "Your website says, 'Every case will be treated with dignity and discretion.' That's all I ask."

I looked into her eyes and said, "Okay."

She seemed to sense my reluctance and started, rushing, "Those bedroom windows are papered-over *twenty-four hours a day*! And the begonias, you didn't *see* him destroy those begonias! I saw how he severed their stalks and shredded their root systems. You don't do that to flowers you've tended for an entire season. Not if you're a person of sound mind."

"Gardening is more challenging for some than others. I love rhododendrons, but I can't keep them alive. I overwater, I under-water. I plant them in the wrong spot."

"Have you ever massacred them in a fit of rage?"

"No." I smiled. "But I've wanted to."

Martha couldn't help returning the smile. But her eyes stayed on Kent Kirkland's house.

I said, "Some men aren't blessed with impulse control. Maybe he was a lousy gardener, he'd tried fertilizing and everything else, and the plants just refused to—"

"But he wasn't a lousy gardener. He was excellent. I think he grew those begonias from seed. He wanted them to be perennials, is my theory, but we're in zone seven—they're annuals here. He couldn't accept them dying off."

Again, I was at a loss. I liked Martha Dodson. She had seemed like a reasonable person, right up until she'd started talking about kidnappings and Venezuela.

She scooted closer on the couch. "You didn't see the rage, Miss McGill. I saw it. I saw him that day. He walked out of the garage with hand pruners, but he took one look at those begonias—leaves browning at the edges, stems tangled like green worms—and flipped out. He turned right around, put away the hand pruners, and came back with clippers."

She mimed viciously snapping a pair of clippers closed.

"Rage is one thing," I said. "Kidnapping is another."

"Of course," Martha said. "That's why I'd like to hire you: to figure out what he might be capable of."

Her pupils seemed to pulse in place.

"I want to help you out, honestly." I took her hand. "I do."

"Is it money? I—I could pay you more. A little."

Saying this, she seemed to linger on my jacket. I'd recently swapped out my boiled wool standby for this slightly flashier one, red leather with zippers. I had no great ambitions about an image upgrade; it'd just felt like time for a change.

"The fee we discussed will be sufficient," I said. Martha had mentioned she was paying out of her own pocket, not from her and her husband's joint account. "My concern is more about the substance of the case. It feels a bit outside my expertise."

She clasped her hands at her waist. "Is it a question of danger? Do you not handle dangerous jobs?"

I balked. In fact, I'd done extremely dangerous jobs before, but only as part of Third Chance Enterprises, the freelance small-force, private-arms team led by Quaid Rafferty and Durwood Oak Jones. We'd stopped an art heist in Italy. We'd saved the world from anarchist-hackers. Sometimes I can hardly believe our missions happened. They feel like half dream, half blockbuster movies starring me. Every couple years, just about the time I start thinking they really might be dreams, Quaid shows up again on my front porch.

"I don't mind facing danger on a client's behalf," I said. "But McGill Investigators isn't meant to replace the proper authorities. If you believe Mr. Kirkland is involved in these disappearances, your first stop should be the police."

"Mm." Martha's face wilted, reminding me of those unlucky begonias. "Actually, it was."

"You spoke with the police?"

She nodded. "Yes. Well, more of a front-desk person. I told him exactly what I've been telling you today."

"How did he respond?"

There was a floor loom beside the couch. Martha threaded her fingers through its empty spindles, seeming to need its feel.

"He said the department would 'give the tip its due attention.' Then on my way out, he asked if I'd ever read anything by J. D. Robb."

"The mystery writer?" I asked.

"Right. He told me J. D. Robb was really Nora Roberts, the romance novelist. He said I should try them. He had a hunch I'd like them."

My teeth were grinding.

I said, "Some men are idiots."

Martha's face eased gratefully. "Oh, my husband thinks the same. I'm a Yancy Park housewife with too much time on her hands. He says Kirkland's just an odd duck. When I told him about the begonias, he got this confused expression and said, 'What's a perennial?'"

I could relate. My first husband had once handed me baking soda when I asked for cornstarch to thicken up an Italian beef sauce. The dish came out tasting like soap. After I traced back the mistake, he grumbled, *Ah, relax. They're both white powders.*

As much as I probably should have, I couldn't refuse Martha. Not after this conversation.

"I suppose I can do some poking around," I said. "See if he, I don't know, buys suspicious items at the grocery store. Or puts something in his garbage that might have come from a child."

Martha lurched forward and clutched my hands like I'd just solved the case of Jack the Ripper.

"That would be amazing!" she cried. "Thank you *so* much! I know this seems far-fetched, but my instincts tell me something's wrong at that house. If I didn't follow through, if it turned out I was right and those little boys..."

She didn't finish. I was glad.

CHAPTER TWO

The state of New Jersey offers private investigator licenses, but I've never gotten one. It doesn't entitle you to much, and you have to put up $250, plus a $3,000 "surety bond." Besides the money, you're supposed to have served five years as an investigator or police officer. Which I haven't.

For all these reasons, my first stop after taking any case involving possible crimes is the local police station. Sometimes the police are impressed enough by what I tell them to assign their own personnel, usually some rookie detective or beat cop.

Other times, not.

"Begonias, huh?" said Detective Art Judd, lacing his fingers behind a head of bushy brown hair. "The ones with the thick, fluffy flower heads?"

"You're thinking of chrysanthemums," I said.

"Nnnno, I feel like it was begonias."

"Not begonias. Maybe peonies?"

"Don't think so," he said. "I'm pretty sure the gal in the garden center said begonias."

I was annoyed—one, at his stubborn ignorance of flowers, and two, that he'd segued so breezily off the subject of Kent Kirkland.

"The only other possibility with a thick, fluffy flower head would be roses," I said. "But if you don't know what a rose looks like, you're in trouble."

Judd's lips curled up below a mustache. "You could be right."

I waited for him to return to Kirkland, to stand and pace about his sparsely decorated office, to offer some comment on the bizarre behavior I'd been describing for the last twenty minutes.

But he just looked at me.

Oh, I didn't mind terribly being looked at. He was handsome enough in a best-bowler-on-his-Tuesday-night-league-team way. Broad, sloping shoulders, large hand gestures that made the physical distance between our chairs feel shorter than it was.

I'd come for Martha Dodson, though.

"Leaving aside what is or isn't a begonia," I said, "how would you feel about checking into Kent Kirkland? Maybe sending an officer over to his house."

He finally gave up his stare, kicking back from his metal desk with a sigh. "The department barely has enough black-and-whites to service the parking meters downtown."

"I'm talking about missing boys. Not parking meters."

"Point taken," he said. "Why didn't Mrs. Dodson come herself with this information?"

"She did. Your front-desk person brushed her off."

The detective looked past me into the precinct lobby.

"They see a lot of nutjobs. You can't go calling in the calvary every time someone comes in saying their neighbor hung the wrong curtains."

"They aren't curtains," I said. "The windows are papered over. Completely opaque."

He rubbed his jaw. I thought he might be struggling to keep a straight face.

I continued with conviction I wasn't sure I actually felt. "I *saw* it. It isn't normal how he obscures that window. Martha thinks it's weird, and it is weird."

"Weird," he said flatly. "Two votes for weird."

"You put those Neighborhood Watch signs up, right?" In response to his slouch, I stood. "You encourage citizens to report anything out of the ordinary. When a citizen does so, the proper response would seem to be gratitude—or, at the very least, respect."

This, either the words or my standing up, finally pierced the detective's blithe manner.

"Okay, I give. You win." His barrel chest rose and fell in a concessionary breath. "It's true, with police work you never know which detail matters until it matters. Please apologize to Mrs. Dodson on behalf of the department. And I'll be sure to have a word with Jimmie."

He gestured to the lobby. "Kid's been getting too big for his britches for a while now."

I thanked him, and he ducked his head in return.

Then he said, "I suppose she thinks one of those boys being held is Calvin Witt."

The boy whose parents had lost track of him.

"Yes," I said. "The timing does fit."

I considered mentioning the scooter, Calvin's Christmas wish, but decided not to. We didn't need to go down the rabbit hole of box shapes and labeling, and whether grown men rode scooters.

Detective Judd looked ponderously at the ceiling. I didn't expect him to divulge information about a live case, but I thought if he knew something exculpatory—that Calvin Witt had been spotted in Florida, say—he might pass it along and save me some trouble.

"I hate to say this, but I honestly doubt young Calvin is among the living." Art Judd smeared a hand through his mustache. "The father gambled online. Mom wanted out of the marriage, bad. She told anybody in her old sorority who'd pick up her call. Both of them meth heads."

"That's disheartening," I said. "So you think the parents..."

He nodded, reluctance heavy on his brow. "It'll be a park, under some tree. Downstream on the banks of the Millstone. Pray to God I'm wrong."

I matched his glum expression, both a genuine reaction and a professional tactic to encourage more disclosure. "Does the department have staff psychologists, people who study these dysfunctional family dynamics? Who're qualified to unpack the facts?"

"Eh." Art Judd flung out his arm. "You do this job long enough, you start recognizing patterns."

This was a common reaction to the field of psychology: that it was just everyday observation masquerading as science, that anyone with a little horse sense could practice it.

I said, "Antipathy between spouses doesn't predict antipathy toward the offspring, generally."

The detective's face glazed over like I'd just recited Einstein's theory of relativity.

"Perhaps I could conduct an interview," I said. "As a private citizen, just to hear more background on Calvin?"

He chuckled out of his stupor. "Good try. You're free to call as you like, but I don't think the Witts are real receptive to interview requests now—with the exception of the paying sort."

I crossed my legs, causing my skirt to shift higher up my knee. "Is there any further background you'd be able to share? You personally?"

His gaze did tick down, and he seemed to lose his first word under his tongue.

"Urb, I—I guess it's all more or less leaked in the press anyway," he said, and proceeded to give me the story—as the police understood it—of Calvin Witt.

Calvin had a lot to overcome. His parents, besides their drug and money problems, were morbidly obese, and had passed this along to Calvin. A social worker's report found inadequate supplies of fresh fruit and lean proteins at the home. They'd basically raised him on McDonald's and ice-cream sandwiches. Calvin had learning and attention disorders. He started fights in school. His parents couldn't account for huge swaths of his day, of his week, even.

"They let him run like the junkyard dog," Detective Judd said. "All we know about the night he disappeared, we got off the kid's bus pass. Thankfully it'd been registered. We know he boarded a bus downtown, late."

I opened my mouth to ask a follow-up.

"Before you get ideas," he said, "no, the route didn't pass anywhere near Martha Dodson's neighborhood. We always cross-check Yancy Park in these cases. That's where the Ferguson place is."

"Ferguson?"

"Yeah. Big rickety house, half falling over? Looks like the city dump. You shoulda passed it on the way."

I shook my head.

"Well," he continued, "that's where the Fergusons live, crusty old married couple. Them and whatever riffraff needs a room. Plenty of crime there. Squalor. The neighbors keep trying to get it condemned."

I definitely didn't remember driving past a place like that. "Were there any witnesses who saw Calvin on the bus? Saw who he was with?"

"Nobody who'd talk."

"Camera footage?"

The detective palmed his meaty elbow. "Have you *seen* the city's transportation budget?"

I incorporated the new information, thinking about Kent Kirkland. He was single according to Martha. Midthirties. He worked from home—something to do with programming or web design, she thought.

Did he have a car? I'd noticed a two-car *garage*, but I hadn't seen inside.

Did he go out socially? To bars? Or trivia nights?

Could he have ridden the bus downtown?

"Martha mentioned another case," I said. "Last summer, I think it was. Another boy in the same vicinity?"

At first, Detective Judd only squinted.

I prompted, "There was some connection to Venezuela. The father was born there, maybe he—"

"Right, that Ramos kid!" Judd smacked his forehead. "How could I forget? Talk about red tape, my gosh. So he's boy number two, is that it?"

I couldn't very well answer "yes" to a question posed like that.

I simply repeated, "Martha mentioned the case."

"Yep. That was a doozy." As he remembered, he walked to a file cabinet and pulled open a drawer. "Real exercise in frustration."

"There was trouble with the Venezuelan government?"

"And how." He swelled his eyes, thumbing through manila folders, finally lifting out an overstuffed one. "I must've filled out fifty forms myself, no joke."

He tossed the file on his desk. Documents slumped from the folder out across his computer keyboard.

I asked, "You never located the boy?"

"Not definitively. We had a witness put him with the paternal grandparents, the day before Dad put the whole crew on a plane."

"Did you interview him?"

"Who?"

"The father."

Detective Judd burbled his lips. "Nope. The Venezuelans stonewalled us—never could get him, not even on the horn. He told some website he had no clue where the kid was, but come on. They took him."

I'd been following along with his account, understanding the logic and sequence—until this. I thought about Zach, my fourteen-year-old, and what lengths I would've gone to if he'd disappeared with his father.

"So you...stopped?" I said.

He stiffened. "We hit a brick wall, like I said."

"Yes, but a boy had been taken from his mother. What did she say? Was she satisfied with the investigation?"

"No." Judd's mouth tightened under his mustache. His tone turned challenging. "Nobody's satisfied when they don't like the outcome."

I tugged my skirt lower, covering my knee.

He continued, "I get fifty-some cases across my desk every week, Miss McGill. I don't have the luxury of devoting my whole day to chasing crackpot theories just because somebody looks angry snipping their flowers."

"Of course," I said. "Which makes me the crackpot."

He closed his eyes, as though summoning patience. "You seem like a nice lady. And look, I admit I'm a Neanderthal when it comes to matters—"

"'Nice lady' puts you dangerously close to pre-Neanderthal territory."

He smiled. In the pause, two buttons began blinking on his phone.

"Pleasant as it's been getting acquainted with you," he said, "I can't commit resources to this begonia guy. Just can't. If you can pursue it without stepping over any legal boundaries, more power to you."

I felt heat rising up my neck. I gathered my purse.

"I will pursue it. Two little boys' welfare is on the line. Somebody needs to."

He spread his arms wide, good-naturedly, stretching the collar of his shirt. "Hey, who better than you?"

The contents of the folder labeled *Ramos* were still strewn over his keyboard. "I don't suppose I could borrow this file..."

"Official police documents?"

"Just for twenty minutes. Ten—I could flip through in the lobby, jot a few notes."

He'd walked around his desk to show me out, and now he stopped, hands on hips, peering down at the file. The top paper had letterhead from the Venezuelan consulate.

I stepped closer to look with him, shoulder to shoulder. Our shoes bumped.

"Or even just this letter," I said. "So I have the case number and contact information for the consulate. Surely there's no harm in that?"

Detective Judd didn't move his shoe. He smelled like bagels and coffee.

He placed his fingertip on the letter and pushed it my way.

"I can live with that."

"Thanks," I said, grinning, snatching the paper before he could reconsider.

CHAPTER THREE

I drove home through Yancy Park, thinking to get a second look at Kent Kirkland's property. As I pulled into the subdivision, I noticed a dilapidated house up the hill, off to the west. It rose three stories and had bare-wood sides. Ragged blankets flapped over its attic windows.

The Ferguson place.

Somehow I'd missed it driving in from the other direction. Art Judd had been right: the place was an eyesore. Gutters dangled off the roof like spaghetti off a toddler's abandoned plate. A refrigerator and TV were strewn about the dirt yard, both spilling their electronic guts.

I made a mental note to ask Martha Dodson about the property. I found it curious she suspected Kirkland instead of whoever lived in this rats' den. Art Judd had mentioned cross-checking Yancy Park. Maybe the police had already been out and investigated to Martha's satisfaction.

I kept driving to Martha and Kent Kirkland's street. I slowed at the latter's yard, peering over a rectangular yew hedge to a house that was the polar opposite of the

Ferguson place. The paint job was immaculate. Gutters were not only fully affixed, but contained not a single leaf or twig. Trash bins were pulled around the side into a nook, out of sight.

Now that I knew the missing boys' backstories, my brain was bursting with scenarios. How would the logistics work if Kirkland *did* have them?

How would he run errands? Did that bedroom door lock from inside? Were the windows reinforced so the boys couldn't bust them out, or soundproofed so they couldn't scream to passersby? How about doctor visits? What happened if they got sick? They must be missing their vaccinations.

I drove on, fully aware that Martha's theory remained a long shot. Any number of factors might explain Kent Kirkland's behavior. Obsessive parents. A brush with instability early in life. Maybe his father had mislaid some check that nearly put the family out on the street, so that now Kent couldn't stomach a single scrap of paper, morsel of food, or flower petal out of place.

Everybody's situation can look bizarre from a distance.

Exhibit 1-A: my own porch half an hour later as I pulled up the driveway. Its front railing—which lay somewhere in between Ferguson and Kirkland on the Needs Paint scale—was lined with stuffed animals. Twenty or twenty-five, ordered smallest to tallest.

I parked my beloved Prius, which I'd bought used as a high-mileage rental, and walked up the porch steps.

My six-year-old, Karen, was just backing through the screen door carrying more stuffies in her arms—and between her fingers, and pinned to her sides, and balanced in the crook of her neck...

"Do you need some help?" I asked.

"No," she said. Then Blue Elephant slipped from her grasp, followed by Hedgie Hedgehog. "Actually, uh, maybe?"

I leaned down and got Blue Elephant and Hedgie in a single scoop, then walked them to the railing. "It looks like you have a preferred order."

"I do," she said, her chin high and smiling—that smile I would've moved mountains for.

We slotted the newcomers in their proper places. Hedgie's height was exactly the same as Paddington's, but Hedgie got the taller, leftward spot because "Paddington has a hat and that's no fair."

I helped Karen ferry another load of stuffies out to the porch. "Why are we doing this, honey?"

"Because Simba peed again," she said, speaking of our litter-box-challenged cat. "They all have to get smell-tested."

Ah yes. That makes sense.

Well, six-year-old sense.

"And you felt like the smell-tests needed to be done outside?"

"Obviously." She rolled her eyes—green, perfect mirrors of my own. "You have to do smell-tests in nature, it's fresher."

I had to concede that nature was, no doubt, fresher than my house.

I pointed to her hair, which was gathered in a pair of uneven clumps. "Want me to redo your ponytails?"

She shook her head vigorously. "Sophie Simpson does her own hair every morning, *by herself.* I'm starting too."

With delicate touches, she gauged the shape of her

hairdo. The left ponytail started near her temple while the right was high, almost a straight-up whale spout look.

"You know how we brush out your hair every night?" I said. "We do that because—"

"I know, I know about brushing out!" She tried pulling some of her right bangs across her forehead to the left ponytail. "This is how I want it."

The tangled mess was turning my stomach a little. That one hair band would need to be cut out with scissors, I thought.

There's a fine line between allowing kids to learn from mistakes, and standing pat as they dig themselves deeper and deeper into the abyss.

"Alright," I said. "I'll let you problem solve. I need to go inside and check on Zach." I gestured to the stuffies. "Can I come back later and help you smell-test?"

"Once I have them all ready. It has to be equal for testing."

"Right," I said. "Equal."

I left her to continue tweaking the stuffies' order. Inside, there was no sign yet of Granny, who was supposed to be watching the kids. Presumably, Zach was around—I'd seen his skateboard leaning against the house.

Now I stood in the middle of the living room surrounded by loose art supplies, library books, mail, a basket of unfolded laundry.

What would Art Judd think of all this?

I scolded myself for the thought. Art Judd wasn't interested in me. I just happened to be in his office, a woman in a skirt, so he'd responded. I could've been a female lawyer, a cop, a secretary bringing him copies.

More importantly, I wasn't interested in him. There

was too much happening in my life. I was scraping to keep the lights on and mortgage paid. Zach's algebra grade was the pits. Karen had a wonderful disposition and imagination, but her interest in reading hadn't sparked like I'd hoped.

My head felt wet. Why did my head feel wet?

I twisted my neck around to check, then got a drop straight in my eye.

The ceiling was dripping.

"Zach!" I shouted, bolting for the stairs.

I took them three at a time, lunging, panting. I dashed through the hall to the bathroom. In my peripheral vision, I caught a glimpse of Zach in his room—checking himself out in a mirror.

I reached the bathroom.

"*Zach*, oh...Zach," I said with a falling heart.

The sink had run over, a small but relentless stream of water flowing from the basin, across the counter, onto the tile below. An array of hair products—gels, sprays, molding muds—was spread across the vanity.

My first step inside sloshed. I banged closed the hot water tap, then hustled to the linen closet for towels—kicking off my sopping shoes.

There were no towels.

I dashed to the hamper. I grabbed the first four dirty towels I saw. Two of my sweaters and a mess of kid socks tagged along in the folds.

"A little help would be nice!" I said, back in the bathroom, tossing everything in my hands onto the minor lake.

I spread the towels on all fours until the area was covered. Then I tamped them down using my hands, elbows, kneecaps, blotting up water, desperate to keep as much as I could from draining through the floor and first-floor ceiling. I hoped this new jacket was waterproof.

I'd just taken my first breath, the mess contained, when Zach appeared in the doorway.

"Whoa," he said. "*Mucho* wet."

"Yeah, *mucho*," I agreed, gathering up the towels that—on the bright side—could go right back into the hamper. "Care to tell me what happened?"

He shifted between feet, eyes searching, a confused series of calculations seeming to occur behind them. His bangs were glossy and wavy and stiff all at once.

"I just moistened my hair." He touched it gingerly. "I know I turned the water off."

With my chin, I indicated the sopping mass of terry cloth. "You definitely did not."

"I *did*!" He threw up his arms in protest. "Karen must've come in here and turned it on when I was in my room."

"She's downstairs arranging her stuffies on the porch."

"Maybe she took a break. Have you been observing her, like, *constantly*? Do you know *for a fact* she wasn't up here messing with the water?"

I closed my eyes. I tried ignoring the angry thrum in my brain and the towels' moisture, which had now penetrated to my bra.

Calmly, I said, "Why couldn't you just use the mirror in the bathroom?"

"Seriously, Mom? This mirror sucks."

"Please stop using that word," I said. "And this is a vanity." I pointed to the ten light bulbs above the mirror. "It's the clearest mirror in the house."

He sneered at his reflection. "It makes my bangs look...off. Unnatural."

He teased them away from his forehead. Half the hairs stayed just where he released them. The other half fell.

If I'd been arguing on the merits, I would've informed him that how his bangs looked in this mirror was how his bangs looked, period.

But I wasn't arguing on the merits. I was arguing with a teenager.

"It's just the angle." I reached up and fixed the fallen hairs. "There. Now they look, you know, normal. Like normal bangs. All set."

He cut his eyes warily at the mirror, but I could see the corners of his mouth relax.

Kids and hair. Ugh.

Now Zach did help me clean up. We finished in the bathroom, then headed downstairs to the living room, where Zach stood on tiptoes pressing paper towels into the ceiling's bloated, blistering paint. We extracted all the moisture we could. The ceiling still had a damp spot sagging a half inch below the rest.

Now it needed paint too.

I asked, "What happened to Granny?"

My seventy-four-year-old grandmother, Eunice, lived with us. When I'd left this afternoon to meet Art Judd, she had assured me she would keep an eye on the place.

Zach said, "She fell asleep."

Shuffling sounded from the stairs, followed by a shrill voice.

"*Nobody fell asleep!*" Granny said. "I shut my eyes, is all. At no point were either of those two young persons left unsupervised."

In her slippers and lavender robe, Granny tottered sourly into the living room. She saw the ceiling.

"Goodness." She blinked. "Molly, you'd better do something about that."

"Yes, Granny." I worked up a smile. "I suppose I'd better."

With a skeletal hand, she gripped my elbow in approval before heading off to watch TV—either cable news or a judge show.

From the porch came a familiar series of *bloops* and *blip-de-whoops*.

"Karen..." I called, starting that way.

Outside, my daughter was hunched in a corner, using her body as a shield as she played on my phone.

"Please hand it over," I said.

"What? I was just trying this game," she said.

"You've 'tried' SparklePopper about a hundred times," I said. "You know you're not allowed on my phone."

"But Sophie Simpson plays her mom's phone all the time."

"That's between Sophie and her mother."

"*She* even texts her mom's boyfriends. She gets to pick out what emojis they use."

"Wonderful." I held out my palm, waiting. "Those must be precious moments when they're deciding between winky face and heart-eyes smiley face."

Karen giggled, but I felt instantly bad about the snark.

I continued, "You know my feelings about electronics. Other families may do it differently, but we are going to interact with each other. I'm raising humans, not button-pushers."

She surrendered the phone.

I participated in smell-testing all her stuffies. Zach and even Granny got into the act, crinkling their faces at those needing enzyme treatment, flashing a thumbs-up at the rest.

Finally, in the few minutes remaining before I needed to start dinner, I flattened the letter from the Venezuelan consulate in front of me on the kitchen table.

It said nothing substantial, basically that the consulate had received the request to compel Esteban X. Ramos to speak with the Hicks County Police Department, and would render a determination as to the request's validity within ninety days.

The letterhead listed two phone numbers, one with a country code and another a toll-free 800 number.

I tried the 800 number first and got an earful of high-pitched screech. Their fax number?

I cringed, tapping out the second number, imagining what Verizon was going to charge me for all these digits. A woman picked up on the fourth ring.

"*Hola, puedo ayudar?*"

"Uh, yes," I said. "I'm calling from the United States, trying to get some information about a missing person case."

A scrape sounded over the line, then the woman's voice got louder like she'd picked up the speakerphone.

"Excuse me, what is your request?" the woman said. "Do you have a name with which you wish to speak?"

I got zip. I tried pressuring the woman to transfer me to someone important, an ambassador or high-placed functionary, but she kept suggesting I "contact my liaison in the United States, who has access to this information."

Having worked switchboard temp jobs for Rainey Personnel during McGill Investigators' many lean periods, I understood the woman's situation. She had no power. She was told little and allowed to reveal even less, dooming her to be shouted at all day.

I thanked her and hung up.

The microwave clock read 4:48. I needed to start dinner. Earlier in the day, I'd been thinking beef Stroganoff. Now I was thinking deli turkey sandwiches.

What am I supposed to do about Kent Kirkland?

The boys' side of the case looked impassable. Venezuela wouldn't talk to me. Calvin Witt's parents were under intense media scrutiny—they weren't going to talk to me.

I thought about calling Durwood Oak Jones, my Third Chance partner. Durwood was surprisingly good with computers and, less surprisingly, excellent at making people answer questions.

I thought about calling Martha Dodson and saying that, on second thought, the case just wasn't for me. I'd tried Detective Judd. I'd called the Venezuelan consulate. If she wanted me to stakeout Kirkland or rifle through his bin on trash-pickup day, I would, but I had to be honest. I doubted much would come of it.

Then I thought about Martha taking the news. Those hazel eyes fixing me hopefully, hands busy with some craft. How deflated she would be.

How when her husband got home and asked how her day had gone, she would smile and say, "Just fine," and not mention her brief foray into hiring a private investigator.

I thought about those boys.

And I decided there was only one thing to do.

"Granny?" I said, grabbing my keys and purse. "You know where I keep the deli turkey, right?"

I was going to Kent Kirkland's house. I was getting inside.

CHAPTER FOUR

I swung by Fowler & Sons on my way to Yancy Park. Gage Fowler, who'd joined the family nursery/hardware store after two tours in Afghanistan, met me before I'd even passed by the potted herb and vegetable offerings up front.

"If it isn't my favorite ironwood tree owner," he said. "Has it leafed out yet?"

I smiled and said the tree had, nicely. Gage had spent a solid hour this spring helping me choose a species that would thrive in a tough location near my foundation.

He smiled back. "What can I do for you?"

I explained my needs. Gage stroked his chiseled jaw as he listened, clearly curious about my interest in such eccentric supplies. I didn't enlighten him.

He walked me through the aisles, talking over the whys and wherefores of various options, asking more about my objectives. I kept my answers polite but vague.

I loved walking through Fowler & Sons. The store smelled

rugged, piney. Flat-stacked goods and a sliding ladder in every aisle created a can-do vibe that made me want to start a project, redo my tub or add shelves in the laundry room. Of course, the presence of Gage and his brothers in blue jeans, drumming their biceps pensively among power tools, didn't hurt.

When I had the right items, Gage checked me out.

"I appreciate your help," I said, swiping my credit card. "And I will let you know how it grows."

He handed over my receipt, squinting.

"The ironwood," I said.

"The ironwood, right!" He wagged his head, reminding me of Durwood's dog, Sue-Ann, shaking water out of her coat. "Please do. You should get a good seven, eight, inches."

I drove next to Yancy Park. It was dusk, that time before exterior lights wink on when houses seem to watch the street with slit eyes. Mailbox posts stiffened. A basketball rolled to a stop at the border of a raised bed. A woman turning left into her driveway waited for me to pass, eyeing the Prius as though I were an interloper—which I suppose I was.

Of all these wary houses, none looked warier than Kent Kirkland's. His privacy fence was tall and dark-stained, each board rising to a spike. The path lights gave off skimpy cones of light like they'd just as soon you tripped and broke your neck as came closer.

Around the edges of that papered-over window, a fuzzy glow escaped. I slowed at Kirkland's driveway. Leaning across the passenger seat, I tried to detect—in the window's fuzzy glow—a shadow or color or sliver of face.

I started to turn in, then thought better of it and parked

on the street. Invading his driveway felt too aggressive. I didn't want to spook Kirkland down a hole.

I had transferred my purchases from Fowler & Sons into an official-looking canvas tote. Now I clutched the tote and walked through the street to Kirkland's drive, taking care not to upset his lawn. Up close, his *Please pick up after your pet* signs had tiny quiver lines that gave them the appearance of shouting.

I walked up the porch steps with the creepy—almost slimy—sensation of being watched. The neighborhood's natural quiet deepened here, the gleam-white spindles and hanging wisteria baskets seeming to shield ambient noise.

Where were all the kids on bikes? The joggers? The robins and jays chirping from the treetops?

Bzzzzzzz.

A bee intruded on the silence, far at first, then close, buzzing my head. I ducked away.

I hate bees. I'm embarrassed to admit that because they're so important to the ecosystem, but I can't help it. If they could just do their wonderful and amazing pollination dance quietly, with no threat of stinging, we'd be friends.

When the buzzing relented, I approached Kent Kirkland's front door. It was preceded not by a screen but by the solid glass of a storm door, even though it was early fall. His doorbell was lighted brass.

I pressed it.

A chime sounded inside. Then, for thirty seconds, nothing.

Was he home? There were lights on in the papered-over bedroom and elsewhere. Had I caught him on the phone? In the middle of dinner?

Threatening one of his captives?

At last, I heard footsteps. Then the sound of dead bolts —more than one—unlocking. I braced myself to meet Kent Kirkland. My research hadn't turned up any pictures —nothing on social media or in the newspaper, no yearbook photos online—so I had no clue what he would look like.

The door opened crisply.

Psychology has plenty to tell us about first impressions. They can be faulty or preternaturally astute. They can endure, or vanish the instant we hear a person's voice or see their smile.

My impression of Kent Kirkland, I knew right away, would endure. One word would remain forever attached to him in my mind: "intense."

"How may I help you?"

He spat more than asked the question, standing ramrod stiff with his face angled back. He wore glasses with thick black frames and a necktie—not loosened at the top. His jaw looked freshly shaved.

"Hello, sir," I said. "I couldn't help noticing how skillfully landscaped your property is. Are those Japanese barberry around the west border?"

Kirkland's fingers kept tight hold of the storm door. "They are."

I took a step back to look, marveling. "Wonderful spot for them. Bravo. So many home gardeners over-plant barberry, but you've confined the bushes to just the right size."

The praise brought a light flush to his face. I reached in my tote, following the plan I'd sketched out mentally before visiting Fowler & Sons, but Kent Kirkland shut me down in the next breath.

"I don't entertain door-to-door solicitors," he said stodgily. "Good day."

He began closing the door. I slipped my knee inside.

"No, no, I'm not here selling anything!" I said. "Not at all, no. I just came..."

That he didn't slam the door on my leg—stopping at the last second—was encouraging. I fingered the seed packets in my tote, stalling.

"The reason I came, you see, came and rang your handy bell here"—I tapped the lighted button like a goof—"was more in an enthusiast-type role."

Kent Kirkland's lips twitched.

"Enthusiast?" he repeated.

My mouth felt drier than meatloaf left twenty minutes too long in the oven. "Yes. My official role is with the Northern New Jersey Horticultural Society." I was warming to the ad-lib. "We're making the rounds with neighborhood gardeners, those who've shown an interest in serious horticulture. Not just plunking some shrubs from Home Depot into holes you dug yesterday. We're looking for people who're truly pushing the bounds of what's possible in our hardiness zone."

The snobby praise—I'm *lucky* if I manage to keep my own Home Depot purchases alive—had the desired effect. Kirkland's eyes, behind those chunky frames, softened.

His words didn't.

"You're asking for money," he said.

"No, I—"

"Everyone who comes to my door wants money. The pitches start differently, but they all end in the same place."

He punctuated this bit of commentary with a tiny,

saccharine smile. I wanted to reach out and yank that necktie even tighter, but I didn't.

Temp work has taught me plenty of life skills, few more useful than the ability to transform a person's naked hostility into positivity. When you're making eight dollars an hour to follow a copy-collate script, then it turns out the script is wrong and you get chewed out for collating in reverse order, it's an ability you simply must have. It's a survival skill.

"Let's start over, shall we?" I said. "My name is Molly. I'm with the Northern New Jersey Horticultural Society. We have some items that may be of interest to you."

Before he could object, I took the seed packets from my tote and fanned them like a deck of cards. I had peonies, bluebells, tiger lilies, forget-me-nots, daisies, and, yes, begonias. Fowler & Sons specializes in exotic species, and each packet had some unique interest—a larger- or smaller-than-typical size, resistance to pests, an unexpected color.

As Kirkland's eyes snagged on the packets, I took the chance to look past him at the foyer. It matched the house's facade. A spotless mirror. Neat, narrow table. Two sets of keys hanging from a magnetic organizer. Shoes out of sight.

Why two sets of keys?

"These peonies can take part shade?" Kirkland said. "And the begonias are winter hardy to zone six?"

I made a mental note to thank Gage, who'd said these varietals would "impress the greenest of green thumbs." He'd been on the money.

"That's correct, zone six," I said.

"Eight is the lowest I've managed to find." Kirkland raised his chin, causing something in his neck to crack. "I tried keeping them through the frost. They didn't cooperate."

Martha's description of the begonia massacre, those green-streaked clippers, came back to me.

I maintained eye contact. "We work with some of the most innovative growers in the state. We're pushing the envelope—with hybridization, with soil enrichments. It's quite exciting."

Kirkland stared at the flowers pictured on the packet. They featured two-tone blossoms and a broad, lush habit.

I said a quick prayer in my head before continuing, "I have some literature on the program. If we could sit down for a moment, I'd be happy to talk you through a few pamphlets."

The suggestion seemed to trip an alarm in Kirkland. His eyes snapped up from the packets as though he were coming out of a trance.

"The dinner hour," he said, "is a strange time to be making the rounds, knocking on people's doors."

I ambled another step inside, hoping for a peek at the living room. The foyer doesn't say much about a person. Nobody spends time in the foyer. A living room, on the other hand, reveals its owner's focus. TV? Cozy fireplace? Infant play mat? A living room anchors its home decor. Warm wood, white paint, beams or vaulted ceilings over-head—all these modes are discoverable in a glance.

Although the kitchen tells even more.

"I do regret the timing," I said. "I'm with my children during the day. I can't get to my work with the horticultural society until my husband gets home to mind the store."

It's a bad habit, but when I'm pressed into a lie, I not infrequently blame the children.

Kirkland looked to my hand. "Husband, you said?"

I turned my bare ring finger around.

Shoot.

"That's right," I said. "I, uh...the dirt. Gardening involves so much digging, so much dirt. I quit wearing the ring."

"And your husband allows it?"

I felt bile coming up my throat. I focused on a stray hair on Kirkland's left cheek that he must've missed with the razor. It was short and squiggly.

It was funny. *Ha-ha,* I thought. *Look at the man and his funny little whisker.* The bile receded.

"He does, yes. He allows it."

Maybe some bitterness crept into my voice because Kirkland said next, "I think it would be best if you left. It's late."

He moved for the door, and I saw my opportunity slipping. *I'm inside. I need to press forward.* Quaid Rafferty, my other Third Chance partner, is fond of saying, "Bad guys like their space. When you get close, make your play—you will not be offered drinks."

Heart pumping, I slipped a hand into my tote and tore the corner off a packet. Then I fumbled my tote sideways, letting its contents spill.

Seeds splashed across Kent Kirkland's wood floor.

"I'm such a klutz!" I said. "Sorry, here, I'll scoop them up."

As I dropped to my knees, Kirkland's face tightened and approached the color of eggplant. He looked down at his shoes, jet-black oxfords that now had a fine spray of seed dust.

Behind my back, I ripped open a second packet.

"Oh no!" I said, showing him the ruptured packets. "If these seeds get mixed up, they're useless. I have to get them into the light, someplace where I can sort. I don't suppose you have a table I could use?"

Kirkland towered over me. Were the cuffs of his slacks trembling?

I said, "A plain old kitchen table would be great."

His jaw sawed back and forth. I wondered what he was thinking. Was he considering snagging a few seeds for himself? Questioning my identity? Deciding how suspicious it would look if he turned down my perfectly reasonable request?

Maybe he wasn't thinking at all. Maybe he was listening —listening to make sure whatever was in the bedroom over the garage wasn't calling for help.

Finally, Kirkland said in a strangled tone, "Follow me."

He pivoted on the ball of his oxford and started for the kitchen. I followed, head buzzing, scooping up the rest of my seeds. I'd succeeded. I'd gotten exactly what I had wanted from him.

So why did I feel like sprinting back out to my car?

CHAPTER FIVE

I walked a step behind Kent Kirkland to his kitchen. I wanted to be scanning the house for any sign of captives, but I found myself unable to look away from Kirkland's back. His dress shirt had parallel creases running from the collar to his center belt loop. The material was stark white and without a wrinkle in sight. He couldn't have leaned back in a chair once all day—much less a comfy couch—and kept creases like that.

"Here's a table," Kirkland said with an impatient gesture. "Will this do?"

The table was wide and clutter free, finished so smartly that I could make out my own strawberry-blond flyaways in its gleaming surface.

"It'll do, yes," I said, and began transferring spilled seeds from my cupped palms onto the table.

I took my sweet time. Without the distraction of Kirkland's freakishly tidy shirt, my eyes roamed the kitchen. Two slate-gray towels were folded in perfect halves over the oven handle. The stainless-steel fridge had no magnets, as expected since stainless steel isn't magnetic (my second husband had tried forcing one on me; I couldn't give up my Food Network recipe calendar and Karen's preschool art), but even his corkboard organizer looked barren. Not a single jotted note, business card, or Post-it.

I thought of our last pastor at First Presbyterian, who'd insisted on an overhaul of sanitary procedures. "Cleanliness is close to godliness," he would remind us, passing out disinfectant wipes at the door to clean our pews. Pews, bathroom limits, the disposable mini-chalices—it had all felt less about God than his own need to control.

The only trace of mess here was an unruly bookshelf under Kent Kirkland's microwave, where a half dozen cookbooks with misaligned edges and spines were pushed in to different depths. I might've guessed he was in the middle of using one except for the giant bag of Tyson chicken fingers on the counter.

Do grown men eat chicken fingers?

It was an honest question. Most men don't cook for the sake of cooking, so frozen food made sense. He could just be nuking one or two—the bags have those convenient Ziploc seals. But there was so much variety now in frozen. When you can have Indian lentils or Portuguese empanadas in ninety seconds, why *chicken fingers*?

Kent Kirkland cleared his throat.

I jerked from looking at the Tyson bag to find him glaring.

He must've just asked me something.

I said, "Pardon?"

"I *asked*," Kirkland said, his Adam's apple bulging the knot of his tie, "whether you needed a glass of water."

It took me a second to register the offer. "Oh! Yes—yes, sure, that'd be perfect."

He turned away, the near eye seeming stuck on me for a beat. Then he found a tumbler and filled it from the refrigerator water dispenser. The stream struck the glass abruptly.

"Your kitchen is immaculate," I said. "But having seen your garden, I would expect nothing less."

Kent Kirkland placed my water on a coaster. He dropped his chin toward my seeds.

"Thank you," I said.

He grumbled, "Welcome," and dropped his chin again.

"I promise it'll only take me a moment," I said. "Let me get myself organized."

I established four piles and starting nudging similar seeds together with the sides of my pinkies. As this required the full use of my eyes, I focused all my mental energy on hearing.

Is that a scraping noise coming from upstairs?

I worked deliberately, giving any hypothetical boys time to make a racket somehow. Kirkland watched with one fist jammed in his side.

I got my piles mixed up together.

"Whoops," I said, faking a rueful frown.

He sighed and stomped forward to help, drilling his fingernails into the tabletop and flicking seeds to their correct places. Tendons bulged in his forearms.

As we sorted together, Kirkland standing and irked, I seated and apologetic, I plotted my next move. Originally I'd planned to get inside by pitching my exotic seeds, but Kirkland's hasty "no solicitors" policy had forced me to improvise.

But he had shown interest in the seeds. Could the plan be resuscitated? Could I somehow massage my Northern New Jersey Horticultural Society story? Making a sale would give me an excuse to return—to deliver the purchased seeds, to check back on their germination or growth.

I hadn't found ironclad evidence of kidnapped boys, but something strange was going on here.

"As I said, I'm here primarily in an enthusiast role," I began, measuring my words. "I will mention, though, that the society makes its specimens available to fellow enthusiasts for a modest fee."

He gave a snickering snort along the lines of *it figures*, but his eyes were unmistakably on the begonia packet—one of the four I hadn't spilled.

I could just hear his gears turning. *Hardy to zone six...think of all I could achieve with a begonia like that...*

He stewed for a minute. Then he asked, "How modest?"

Every muscle in my face wanted to smile. I stopped them.

"Quite, given the quality." I thought back to the most I'd paid for a seed packet—and tripled it. "Twenty-four dollars."

His face went from eggplant to bright red. "That's outrageous."

I considered the hardy begonias' image admiringly. "The seeds are organic. And these aren't easy specimens to cultivate. You know how drug companies have to charge high prices to recoup their initial research costs?"

Kent Kirkland gave no indication that he did, teeth gnashing.

I said, "They invest so much in making the scientific discoveries that in order to be profitable—"

"Very well," he cut in. "As we established before, it is the dinner hour. I expect you'll be on your way."

As he stood priggishly, I considered slashing my price. *Wait! I forgot about our low, low introductory rate.*

But I'd already strained credulity past all reasonable bounds. I needed to bail, harvesting whatever information I could on my way out.

"Certainly." I nodded to his bag of chicken fingers. "I apologize for delaying your enjoyment of those, uh..."

His eyes followed mine to the counter. "Chicken tenders?"

"Yes! Tenders, fingers. What's the difference, an inch or two of width? But you're eating tenders tonight, not fingers."

This came out more macabre than I'd wanted.

"Great choice," I added. "Pair them with rice and a veg, and everyone's happy, right?"

He didn't acknowledge my praise or respond to the implied plurality of "everyone." He just glared at me.

I try hard to give people the benefit of the doubt, but I have to admit, I felt intense dislike for Kent Kirkland. He was so quick to be exasperated, to assume his superiority over you—over everybody. He seemed like the type who walked around all day feeling grateful to be who he was instead of some unworthy loser.

That doesn't make him a kidnapper, I reminded myself. *Focus on facts, not personality.*

I stood from the table. "We do a lot of those pasta packets at my place. The kids get bored with rice."

"Fascinating," Kirkland said.

"And potatoes, potatoes are always an option," I said. "You've got scalloped, julienned...potatoes O'Brien...and almost all of them now you can make straight from a box."

These heavy hints were directed toward the pantry, whose door was ajar. I'd been trying to see inside and caught a sliver of yellow-orange box, but I couldn't make out a label.

Triscuits?

Ritz crackers?

The difference was significant.

If a kitchen revealed much about a person, the pantry was practically their diary, full of one's innermost thoughts and dreams. Every fridge has your milk, your eggs, your apples and block cheddar cheese, but pantries vary widely according to each household's unique nutritional needs.

If Kirkland were feeding two boys, he would need certain items: primarily, carbs and calories. An entire shelf of my own pantry was dedicated to Zach's chips, crackers, and various bars—protein, granola, cereal.

"Your knowledge of cheap processed starches is impressive," Kirkland said. "I would've expected a member of a horticultural society to do more scratch cooking."

He started for the front door, clearly intending me to follow.

I had the panicked feeling of opportunity vanishing. I hadn't sold him the seeds or created any reason to come back.

There's no way he's letting me back inside this house.

Ever.

"Did you know," I said, "that the pantry is a tremendous resource for gardeners?"

Kirkland said flatly, "You don't say."

I ignored his lack of enthusiasm. "Vinegar...powdered milk...once you start looking, you find natural fertilizers everywhere!" I took a step. "We play this game at our monthly meeting, 'What's in Your Pantry?' It really is tons of fun—"

"I expect it's riveting," he said. "Be that as it may." His eyes cut to the foyer.

Again, I felt desperate. I thought about those two boys. I said their names in my head. *Calvin Witt. Jhonny Ramos.* I thought about them cowering before this man for weeks and months.

I never watch those missing-child melodramas on TV, but now I found myself thinking about the terrible things they could be enduring. What sort of restrictions might Kent Kirkland impose? Mealtimes governed by stopwatch? Maniacal hygiene regimes involving steel wool and lye soap?

I glanced back to the kitchen table and saw my un-drunk glass of water. And my purse.

"Thank you for your time," I said. "I'll collect my things and go."

Kirkland made a guttural noise of agreement.

I walked back to the table, took a gathering breath, and —thinking again of Calvin and Jhonny—gripped my purse by its strap and pulled it off the table.

The water glass came with it.

"*Aagh*, you imbecile!" Kirkland roared as pieces of glass sprayed across his hardwood. "How could you be so clumsy? *So stupid?*"

Even though I was in shoes, I instinctively kept my feet in place so as not to step on glass.

"Oh my," I said, "I can't believe that happened." Then,

unable to stop myself: "I didn't realize you'd set the glass so near the edge of the table."

His eyes grew to consume most of their thick frames. "That water was *nowhere near* the edge!"

I scrunched my face, apologetic. "I kinda think it was."

He waited out an inner Vesuvius moment, trembling to the tips of his ears. I squatted and began picking up glass shards.

"Don't!" he commanded. "Next thing, you'll cut yourself and I'll be stuck cleaning blood off the floor too."

His emphasis made it clear the hassle of cleanup outweighed any health risk to me.

Obediently, I stood up. I placed two wet shards on the table.

We looked at each other. Kirkland's anger made me think of a hard boil, how the water bubbles shrink after you lower the heat, becoming a single roiling surface of fury.

"Honestly, I don't mind cleanup duty," I said. "It's twenty percent of motherhood. If you'll just point me to your mop."

But Kirkland waved me off and said he would handle it, stomping from the kitchen.

I wasted only a second enjoying his absence, then got to work, tiptoeing over glass to the pantry. I coaxed the handle just past the frame's magnetic reach and let the door drift open.

I looked inside. Kirkland's pantry was exquisite, blue pasta boxes arrayed like soldiers at attention, bins of loose grains categorized and labeled—*Rice, Quinoa, Oats (rolled), Oats (quick)*. His olive, sesame, and vegetable oils were all the same brand and faced forward in a dedicated Tupperware.

My adrenaline was stalled momentarily by a profound peace, the harps of organizational heaven playing from the recesses of my brain.

Then I saw the granola bars.

The bars' layout was as meticulous as the rest, horizontal boxes stacked tallest to shortest with spines facing out. My eyes almost breezed right by—until the top box.

Bright Ones.

Bright Ones was a new brand of kid-size mini bars advertised as "delivering whole grains and omega-3 fatty acids for your child's most precious resource: her brain." The *O* in the logo was gray with scalloped ridges oriented into a grin, smiley brain matter.

I had avoided Bright Ones myself, refusing to reward some advertising executive's naked appeal to parental insecurity. Also, a lot of their flavors had almond butter, which Zach hates. Bright Ones were clearly intended to be wedged into crowded lunch boxes or rationed out—"Fine, promise you'll eat a good dinner and you can have *one*"—to hangry children.

There was no earthly reason for Kent Kirkland to have Bright Ones bars in his pantry. Forget about the marketing —he'd have to eat four of them to make a decent snack.

From the hall, I heard a rustle. I scrambled back to the kitchen table and, ripping paper towels off a dispenser, made a show of blotting water up off the floor.

Kirkland appeared in the doorway. His necktie seemed tighter, and he held a broom stiffly—like that *American Gothic* farmer and his pitchfork. He took one step toward the mess, then stopped.

The pantry door.

I hadn't closed the pantry door.

His eyes shot to me. *Should I try explaining? Make some excuse, say I'd been looking for, what, a bag to put the glass in?*

No. Flailing wouldn't help. I had to pretend nothing was awry. Maybe Kirkland would think the wind had done it, or that he'd nicked the handle himself on his way out.

I was holding a sopping wad of paper towels. Water dripped between my knuckles. I cupped my other hand, trying to contain it but failing.

Each *plop* made my stomach seize.

As Kirkland glared at me, I thought about my own danger. If he really was a kidnapper—a man who held children against their will—could he take me too? Would I have to fight him for my life?

And I found that the longer I considered this possibility, the less afraid I felt. I'd battled supervillains in my work with Quaid and Durwood. Fabienne Rivard, the French heiress and richest woman in the world who kept Cristiano Ronaldo for a boy toy. Igor Bbeschlov, whose army of hooligans had tried to detonate all twenty Premier League stadiums on the queen's birthday.

Was I going to let this narrow man, with his creased shirt and fussy pantry, stop me? With two boys' lives at stake?

I thought about the parents, who'd taken the blame for their kids' disappearance. I thought about the Bright Ones bars. I thought about Martha Dodson, who'd been told by the police to read something by J. D. Robb.

And now I didn't care about the wrath of Kent Kirkland, this murderous glare he was aiming at me.

I didn't care. I was getting a look at that upstairs bedroom.

CHAPTER SIX

K ent Kirkland demanded, "Why is my pantry open?"
I glanced toward the open door.

"That there?" I said. "That's your pantry?"

He re-gripped the broom handle, a tendon bulging in his neck. "No, it's the entrance to my incinerator."

His delivery was so brusque that I missed the sarcasm at first.

"Ha. Incinerator, right," I finally said.

I was still holding the dripping paper towel. I looked around the kitchen as though for a trash can. Kirkland snatched the mess from me and slammed it into a slide-away bin underneath the sink. Then he scowled at the fine dribble his hasty move had left on the floor.

"I'll ask again," he said, "who opened my pantry?"

That wasn't exactly what he'd asked, but I decided splitting hairs at this point wouldn't help my cause.

What could I say to get into that bedroom? What excuse could there be for going upstairs?

"Your cookbooks," I said, gesturing to the unruly

arrangement I'd noticed before. "They have a different, uh, organizational structure than the rest of your home."

Kirkland refused to be distracted. "Books deserve to be free. Now, once more. Who opened my pantry?"

I tripped a moment over his odd phrase about what books "deserved," then recovered to dial up a clueless expression.

"Not me," I said. "Is it possible you opened it yourself? Maybe nicked the handle on your way out."

"No," he said. "That is not possible."

"Just with your elbow? Maybe the very tip and you didn't realize?"

He shook his head indignantly. "That door was closed when I left the room to get supplies—supplies to clean up *your* mess."

To punctuate the point, he thrust his index finger at me. Reflexively I took a half step back and heard glass crunch.

Which gave me an idea.

The two shards I'd gathered earlier were still on the table where I'd set them. Now I shuffled that way and positioned my hips to hide the shards, drumming my hand casually along the tabletop.

"Well, however it got opened," I said, "it's marvelous. Do you ever watch that TV show where the pair of women come and make a project of organizing some family's pantry?"

"If you're insinuating I had professional help, I assure you—"

"They only help out families," I interrupted. Then, holding his gaze: "You send in a video about how disastrous your situation is—macaroni loose, tipped-over baking soda in the back. Maybe you film your kids shoving everything to the ground as they're digging around for a bar."

Kirkland breathed out his nose.

I added, "A *granola* bar."

He pointedly ignored this and stepped toward me. For a second, I thought I'd overplayed my hand and he was attacking. Then he stopped and began sweeping glass into his dustbin.

Behind my back, I picked up one of the shards—the larger of the two. I edged my thumb around it, determining the sharpest side.

How effective would it be as a knife?

I hoped it wouldn't come to that.

Palming the shard, I walked a few steps away under the pretense of giving him space. I needed to act. Once Kirkland had finished cleaning, he would insist on my leaving. He might insist anytime, just glance up from his painstaking broom work and bark at me to get the hell out and never return.

By feel, I found the shard's sharpest point. I positioned it against the center of my opposite hand as Kirkland swept between tiles, grimacing, teasing out debris. I always run the vacuum over a broken-glass cleanup at the end to be safe, but he seemed like the type to insist on getting it all without help from an appliance.

Again, I said the names inside my head.

Calvin Witt.

Jhonny Ramos.

I raked the shard across my skin.

"Ow, *shoot!*" I cried.

I dropped the shard—not an act, it really hurt—and looked down. My palm had a fresh line a quarter inch across. For an instant, it was just a gap in my skin and I had the fantastical thought I could hold my hand like this, just so, and nothing would spill.

Then red rushed in from the surrounding flesh.

I pressed my good hand into my bad to staunch the flow, but my thumb was too small. Blood leaked around the side and dripped onto the hardwood.

It took Kirkland a few seconds to notice, wrapped up in his cleaning and seemingly undisturbed by my shriek.

When he did notice, he railed, "I *told* you! I told you you were going to cut yourself, for the love of..."

He slammed his dustpan down and hustled for paper towels.

"I—I was only trying to help," I said. "I didn't think the pieces would be so sharp."

Now I had my entire off-hand pressed against the cut. The bleeding had stopped, and good thing because I'd just started getting that helium-ish feeling that I might faint. Still, an egg-size pool of blood had already dripped onto the floor.

Kirkland looked from the broken glass to my blood, then back to the glass. His mouth quivered like he wanted to cry or scream or bite the head off a rat.

I said, "Could I trouble you for a Band-Aid?"

This could go one of two ways. Some people keep their Band-Aids upstairs in the linen closet. If Kirkland did, then I could follow him upstairs and—while he was hunting through old eye drops and gauze wraps—steal a peek into that papered-over bedroom.

Other people keep them in the downstairs half bath. If Kirkland did that, then I'd wait for him to disappear before hurrying upstairs. That scenario was trickier. He might hear me. The half-bath might be too near the staircase.

Naturally, Kent Kirkland kept his Band-Aids in neither place.

"I'll get one," he snapped, walking to a short cabinet beside his refrigerator. "Stay where you are."

The cabinet contained three bins. Kirkland removed the center one and, turning his back on me, began sifting through.

Band-Aids in the kitchen? Why so accessible, did he cut himself chopping onions a lot? Or were they for other clumsier occupants?

Kent Kirkland had the Band-Aids now, an economy-size tin that—again—no lone grown-up should need. He reached inside.

I have to move. I have to make it happen.

I said, "I'll just real quick rinse off in your bathroom."

And I pointed to the hall with my good hand, releasing pressure from my cut. Blood started flowing again and Kirkland was answering and I was feeling helium-ish again, but none of it mattered.

I ran. From the kitchen, through the hall, breathlessly for the stairs—I imagined Calvin and Jhonny bunched beside each other with their ears to the door, listening, hoping. I caught a glimpse of the half-bath downstairs. I ignored it. I pounded up the stairs, quads burning like I was in the homestretch of Boody Burn Boot Camp, those six a.m. torture sessions my closest friend, Jennie, had talked me into.

Floorboards groaned behind me. Kirkland was moving.

But I was moving faster. I covered the last three stairs in a single leap. At the landing, I got confused—*wasn't the garage behind me?*—but reoriented myself quickly. No, the garage was ahead. The door I wanted was right here, the first one.

I turned the knob with my cut hand and felt instant runaway pain, like I'd grabbed the handle of a skillet in a four-hundred-degree oven.

What was my plan for the boys? Kirkland was on my heels. I would have to find a weapon—quickly.

Could we overcome him, the three of us? Should we break the window and punch out the paper and scream to somebody on the street, anybody?

The door was strangely sticky in its frame and wouldn't budge. First I thought it was locked or barred, but when I put my shoulder into it, it gave.

I staggered inside and barreled into a folding table covered in Dixie cups. Half the cups scattered to the floor with me, spilling something brown. A folding-arm light crashed down on my head. The air was earthy, thick.

When I'd recovered to sit up, I saw the table was the first of nine. I was in a grow room.

CHAPTER SEVEN

And not even a marijuana grow room, with that skunky smell and fans of serrated leaves. There was a table of bell pepper seedlings, of inverted tomato plants, of feathery baby asparagus—I couldn't make out labels on the other tables.

I scrambled back to the hall on all fours. My cut hand left palm prints on the cream carpet, smears of swirled blood and soil. At the top of the stairs, I met a pair of black oxfords.

"*What,*" Kent Kirkland began, his voice tremulous. "*Have. You. Done?*"

He towered over me, arms crossed.

"I—I'm sorry, that..." I gestured to the trashed grow room. "That isn't your bathroom."

His eyes blazed ahead at the toppled seedlings, at my bloody palm prints, then down the steps at the trail of red I'd left rushing up here.

On my Cleanup Catastrophe Scale, which goes from small-clear-liquid-spill (one) to widespread-encrusted-feces-or-vomit (ten), this was an eight. Cream carpet should be illegal.

"No," Kirkland said, "it most certainly is not my bathroom. My bathroom—or rather, the bathroom I would have directed you to, had you politely asked—is on the ground floor."

I bobbed my head contritely. "If you have some, white vinegar works on blood. You'll want to let it sit for—"

"Hydrogen peroxide," he said, already pulling down a jug at the linen closet. "Bloodstains require hydrogen peroxide."

He removed the jug's top with a practiced twist and poured some into a brush with a built-in dispenser. Then he replaced the jug on its shelf.

That's an awful lot of hydrogen peroxide.

Kirkland dropped to one knee and scrubbed, gouging bristles through the carpet fibers until they regained their original color.

It made sense to hurry before the stains set, of course, but I felt unnerved that he'd stopped harassing me to leave. It seemed as though he'd accepted my presence, like some housefly you chase and chase and finally give up trying to swat.

Until the next time it lands.

I spotted the Ferguson place out the hall window. Its gutters were dangling, shingles sloughing off the roof.

"That house up there, the rundown one," I said, hoping to distract from my mess. "It seems out of character for the neighborhood."

Kirkland scrubbed harder. "What it is is disgraceful. The city should've torn it down years ago."

"How long has it been...overlooked?"

He sneered at my word choice. "Decades. The place is a petri dish for filth and debasement."

"Who owns it?"

As I asked this, the crown of Kirkland's head—which had been bobbing as he scrubbed—stilled.

He answered without looking up, "A pair of devils. Cancers on the community."

I recalled what Art Judd had said about the Fergusons. Had Kirkland butted heads with them at city council meetings? Had he organized petitions to have them ousted?

Whatever the case, the subject had successfully distracted him. I'd redirected him with my questions, turning myself into a co-inquisitor rather than the target of his anger.

But anger is a volatile mode—his switch could flip any moment.

"Oh look, the bleeding stopped," I said, raising and quickly lowering my hand—because it hadn't stopped. "You've got a method here, I can see. I'll show myself out."

I started downstairs without waiting for an answer. I took steps two at a time, stretching out but also flexing my knees to soften each landing. My jaw tightened; my ears tuned for Kirkland's pursuit. I heard none.

I made the bottom of the stairs, still hearing nothing but bristles against carpet. Kirkland was consumed in cleanup. I dashed into the kitchen for my purse, leaving the torn seed packets, and bolted outside.

The sky had gone full dark. After Kirkland's house, the night air was sudden and sweetly cold in my lungs. I hurried through the front yard to my car. A robin skittered away from the right rear wheel.

A tween girl was riding a bike on the opposite sidewalk. She smiled at me.

Thoughtlessly, I waved back with my injured hand. The girl's smile flipped to a frown, and she leaned hard into her pedals.

I slammed the car into gear and drove away. I parked two blocks down and around a corner, well out of sight from Kirkland's house. Then I found a new Band-Aid in the glove compartment and staunched my bloody hand.

I sat and thought. My pulse gradually slowed to normal. *What just happened?*

I had invaded a man's home on false pretenses, snooped in his pantry, and forced my way into a perfectly innocent grow room—bloodying his pale carpet along the way.

Could Kirkland press charges? What happened if he reported me, if the police tracked me down? I had just been making wild accusations to a detective; any accusation of investigatory overreach would seem credible.

What got into my head? The spilled seeds, the water, cutting my hand intentionally—I'd acted possessed. I'd acted like Durwood, who maintains an ad in *Soldier of Fortune* soliciting "injustices in need of attention," and prizes righteousness above all else.

But I hadn't been right. I'd deceived myself, twisted every shred of evidence into proof.

It was tempting to chalk up the mental breakdown to Jhonny and Calvin, to say I'd only done it because I was a mother and kids were involved. But that didn't explain it— not fully. McGill Investigators had pursued missing children before. I'd kept my cool even with such high stakes, in the face of terrible possibilities. I'd never lost control like this.

I sat crunched forward in my car, head against the steering wheel. The Prius felt cramped, confining, just like Granny always complained.

This year was supposed to be easy. Society had finally recovered from the Anarchy, that dark period where the world's data had disappeared, which I'd played a part in ending with Third Chance Enterprises. We didn't have to worry about unchecked motorcycle gangs, or having sprinkler pipe ripped out of our lawns for scrap, or whether somebody would steal Maine.

Our problems were going to be smaller, simpler. Zach's algebra. Karen's reading progress. We were going to embrace our hard-fought normality and roar into post-Anarchy life with a fresh appreciation for all we had.

Only those small, simple problems turned out to be stubborn.

And things we thought we had, we didn't.

After saving the planet, Quaid Rafferty and I had enjoyed five fantastic months together before he jetted off to Ibiza with Sergio Diaz, the mayor of New York City. "I gotta help him blow off some steam," Quaid explained. "A week of sun and surf, then I'm back your way better'n ever."

Predictably, one week turned into three. When Quaid returned, we had more good times—a campout under the stars at Speedwell Lake, introducing Zach to driving (gulp) in parking lots. Quaid surprised Karen and her soccer team with a blowout party at The Bounce Palace.

Then, in July, he took on a sidehustle operation for Greenpeace, helping stop inhumane experiments on Andean condors.

"It's a moral imperative," he said. "I can't sit still knowing these noble creatures are in peril."

I don't know if there were other women during these absences. I believe he was happy with me. We were happy together—I know that for a fact. But the happiness wasn't durable. It was like that nitroglycerin-derived euphoria serum Quaid and Durwood had found in the depths of Corazon Uhr's jungle fortress: lovely, perfect, and gone the moment outside forces breached its fragile shell.

Karen asked me during the Greenpeace operation when the Rainbow Cheetahs, her soccer team, could go back to The Bounce Palace. "Mr. Quaid said he'll take us anytime we want!"

I looked into her eager eyes, and knew I had to end it.

Since then, I'd felt adrift. It wasn't only that I was staring down my late thirties without a life partner, without any vision of my long-range post-kiddos world. I'd lost faith in my own judgment. My septuagenarian grandmother had warned me off Quaid on day one of the Anarchy mission. She'd seen through his silky words—and I hadn't.

Now here I was infiltrating a stranger's house, slashing my own flesh in pursuit of some wild theory about missing boys?

I gripped my key fob and breathed, my head still against the steering wheel. The car smelled like peanut butter.

I needed to go home. I needed to toss my purse onto the coffee table and collapse on the couch, and assess. And figure out how to regain control.

A hard knock sounded on the driver-side window.

CHAPTER EIGHT

I startled out of my thoughts, looking in the direction of the knocks.

It was Martha Dodson.

"Hi Molly, *hi!*" she said through the glass. "I'm so glad we bumped into you. I found something else to show you!"

She was out with Ziggy, wearing hard-soled slippers and the same cardigan as before. I joined them for the last leg of their walk back to Martha's house. I worried about being spotted by Kent Kirkland, but between the dark and our approach from the opposite side, we made it there without trouble.

Inside, Martha unclipped Ziggy's leash and rushed off to find her new evidence.

I was full of dread, hating the news I had to give Martha —not just about that room over Kent Kirkland's garage, but about my own involvement in the case.

Martha returned with a printout, beckoning me to a room off the kitchen.

"He has an alternative identity online!" she said. "'Knut Terwilliger.'"

I followed her to the room, which was dominated by a bulletin board of tacked-up notes, pictures, and newspaper articles—the kind detectives assemble in television crime dramas. The sheer volume of material made it easy to imagine how she'd talked herself into her initial theory of Kirkland holding two boys hostage.

Now Martha explained she'd been kicking around the internet and discovered a series of extremely judgy reviews for Yancy Park businesses.

"...nothing but negative, negative, and more negative." She tapped printouts on her bulletin board. "'The complimentary soup was cold. The salad was overdressed.' 'Poor excuse for a handyman, arrived 11:07 for a scheduled eleven-o'clock appointment.' It was such an odd name that I just had to—"

"Martha," I interrupted, closing my eyes, "we need to go back and revisit some of our basic assumptions—"

"—know who was behind them. I mean, Mike's been out to grease my gaskets, and I never felt taken advantage of."

A section of the bulletin board labeled *Reviews/Knut Terwilliger* included two pictures with a privacy fence identical to Kent Kirkland's in the background.

"See?" Martha clicked away the point of a pen she'd been holding. "Now why wouldn't he put his true name to these reviews? Why the alias?"

My eyes traveled the room. Besides the board, with its cork backing and tacks connected by colored yarn, there was an elliptical machine, a clothes-drying rack, and something long and skinny leaning against the wall in one corner.

"Martha!" I said. "Please tell me you didn't buy a gun as part of this."

"No, no," she said. "Willard does a little deer hunting. He usually keeps it locked in the safe, but the season's about to start this weekend."

That was reassuring.

She continued, "But what do you think about Knut Terwilliger? Doesn't it seem fishy?"

"A bit," I agreed, "although not completely surprising. Listen, Martha. We need to talk. Right before I came here, I was—"

"Oh Lord, your hand!" Martha recoiled at the Band-Aid. The gauze pad had become saturated, leaking into the beige fabric. "Where did you get *that*?"

I held my hand palm-up between us. "At Kirkland's house."

I gave her the full story, from my horticultural society spiel, pitching him on fancy organic flower seeds; to establishing the Guinness record for world's clumsiest house guest; to that bedroom over the garage.

"It's a grow room," I said.

Martha's hazel eyes flashed. "What kind of sicko keeps underage hostages in a room with marijuana plants?"

I took Martha's two quaking hands and pressed them together. Then I looked at her steadily. "There weren't any hostages. Only plants."

The news spread down her face, rounding her eyes, causing one nostril to twitch and her mouth to go slack.

"That's, er, quite a twist," she said. "He must be keeping them in the basement."

She began nodding willfully. "Of course—all these houses in Yancy Park have basements. A basement would be easier to soundproof. And with no windows, he wouldn't have to worry—"

"We're grasping here."

"No, we're not!"

"Yes, we are," I said. "The papered-over window was central to our theory, to this idea something atypical was going on in the Kirkland home. Now that we've explained it, the home's not so atypical."

Martha peeked back at her bulletin board. As my words sank in, she seemed to occupy a smaller and smaller space. The energy she'd tapped my windshield with moments ago had gone.

I suggested, "Shall we go sit in the living room?"

She nodded absently and led us from the room, through the hall, to the couch. I sat in the middle. She took the end closest to her floor loom.

Do it now, I told myself. *Stretching things out is nothing but cruelty.*

The only way to break up is quickly. Quickly and with blinders on. I learned this the hard way in college, when Todd Dixon had wheedled me off my conviction—*but hadn't it been fun at the Sig-Ep party?* and *I'll cut out the farting,* and *whatever, I don't have to watch basketball twenty-four seven*—and I'd ended up wasting six more weeks on him.

"That loom of yours is marvelous," I found myself saying. "Do you have to condition the wood, oil it?"

"Just once a season," Martha said. "My brother built it for me."

"Wow. About the best thing my brothers built me was a

pillow fort, right after they finished slugging me with them."

She chuckled.

Quit stalling. You're only making it worse.

"Is he a carpenter?" I said. "He must build things for a living."

"He wanted to," Martha said. "He died in high school."

This brought conversation to a screeching halt. *Nice job.* On top of my imminent client breakup, now I'd uncovered a sibling lost tragically young.

Still, I needed to do this.

"That's awful, I'm so sorry," I said. "But about the case, Martha. I've got to be honest. I've got to level with you."

I pressed my heels into the carpet, digging deep for resolve. Before I could speak the fatal words, a chain-grinding ruckus sounded through a wall to our right: a garage door opener.

Martha's face changed—for better or worse, I couldn't tell.

A man burst in, saying, "Howie Sorensen did it again, Mar. You're not going to believe it, but I swear it's true. He stole my sandwich outta the break room fridge—"

He broke off seeing us together on the couch.

"Willard," Martha said, rising, "this is Molly, the woman I mentioned. The one who's investigating those missing boys."

Willard Dodson laid his briefcase against an ottoman. He looked sweaty from the commute, individual strands of his comb-over wet.

He said, "Private investigator, are you?"

That was a vast simplification given my experience, but I let it slide.

"Yes."

He nodded with a knowing air. "I'm an insurance agent. I work with clients, talk with clients. Like yourself. Try to understand their needs."

As he spoke, Willard paced the room and gestured expansively.

"I spend most of my time in the field," I said. "Gathering evidence."

He smirked. "Evidence. So you've been out getting evidence on Melvin and, uh..."

"Calvin and Jhonny," Martha supplied.

Willard flubbed his lips. "Right, them. You found a bunch of evidence, huh?"

I considered my response. I was fully aware that I'd been about to drop Martha as a client based on the evidence, but in this moment, I felt the case deserved a more nuanced presentation.

"Quite a lot of evidence," I said. "Mr. Kirkland, the man your wife suspects of—" I dipped my head gravely. "Has a number of bizarre aspects. I got a look inside his pantry and found he keeps it stocked with Bright Ones granola bars."

"*He does?*" Martha exclaimed.

Her husband was nonplussed. "Granola bars. And?"

"And," I continued, mentally digging through my harrowing visit, "he keeps unnatural stocks of hydrogen peroxide on the premises."

Willard flinched, suddenly not bored. "Hydrogen pero-per*oxide?* What is this guy, building a bomb?"

I looked coolly to Martha. She looked coolly back.

To her husband, she said, "Molly has only just started her investigation."

"That's right," I said. "I don't believe in jumping to

conclusions. All you can do as a PI is keep asking questions, keep following the evidence."

My vanilla statement seemed to dull Willard's alarm. Maybe he was remembering his wife using hydrogen peroxide after one of their kids suffered a bad scrape, or drifting back to high school science—rethinking his snap assessment that it was some scary exotic chemical.

Maybe we'd just exhausted his attention span.

"People are bonkers all right," he said through a yawn. "Mar, you mind if I catch twenty minutes on the railroad before din? That trestle bridge never would sit flush for me last night."

Martha told him to go ahead. Dinner wouldn't dry out, cheese and poblano enchiladas.

Willard smacked his lips.

To me, he said, "Lemme know if you need directions getting home. Yancy's not a grid, we got some screwy roads that run diagonal. Easy to get lost."

"I'm sure it is," I said. "Thanks for the offer."

As he disappeared to work on his railroad, Martha faced me with a beaming expression. Now that she'd mentioned them, I smelled poblanos—that rich, slightly smoky tang.

"Where do we go next?" she asked. "Should we try to get into his basement? Or go straight to the police and tell them about the Bright Ones bars?"

I paused to imagine Art Judd absorbing that detail, being told here was my proof Kirkland had Calvin and Jhonny. Probably he would just look at me and say nothing.

Definitely he would stroke his mustache.

"Not just yet," I said. "The granola bars are interesting, but they're more of a supporting detail. We need to tie Kirkland to one of the victims more directly."

Martha accepted this with a studied frown.

"I understand," she said. "At least we're making progress, right? Just tell me what you need. If it's help going through his garbage, or more money, I'll try. I don't have a lot, but I'll try. Anything to help those boys."

I gathered my purse and keys, realizing I had painted myself into a corner. I couldn't drop the case after what I'd said in front of her husband. I couldn't humiliate her like that.

We were stuck together.

At least you haven't heard Martha Dodson fart yet, I thought.

CHAPTER NINE

I considered the case fresh. Ideally, I would've investigated Calvin and Jhonny's disappearances in their own right and judged for myself, impartially, whether they pointed to Kent Kirkland. For several days, I tried this straight-and-narrow approach. I scoured online sources for details and followed up any and all curiosities. I located Calvin's fourth-grade teacher, who'd been quoted as saying he "exhibited signs of distress." I called around to businesses in Venezuela operated by Jhonny's grandparents, fishing for some talkative maid or butler.

But the police had covered this ground. Calvin's teacher sighed and said his "distress" had been the same since Mr. Holt had him in second grade. *How many times did she have to explain?*

Which left me right back where I'd started: with Kirkland.

I didn't take Martha up on her offer to help me inspect her neighbor's trash, but I did do it myself four times over the course of the next two weeks. I would sneak over after my kids' bedtime on collection nights and pore over his shredded receipts, vacuum canister dumps, and unrecyclable plastic overwraps.

Thankfully he used small bags and threw out very little to begin with. I didn't see a single food scrap, which made me think he was composting—logical for a gardener. I didn't see candy wrappers or crumpled juice boxes. I didn't see Bright Ones foil either. Maybe he'd bought them by accident.

I surveilled Kirkland's house at different times of day. If he left, I would tail him at a safe distance of two or three blocks, edging into the next lane to observe Kirkland's driving. His off-white sedan kept fastidiously to the speed limit and obeyed all traffic laws.

Today I was sitting in the Shop-All parking lot, waiting for Kirkland to emerge from a grocery run. I hadn't slept well—Karen had woken me twice after nightmares—and my eyelids kept sagging, blurring my view of customers streaming in and out of the huge box store.

My mind drifted back to the last time I'd been at Shop-All, posing as a member of the Blind Mice. I'd been crouched in *Pickles and Olives*, watching in horror as Josiah, the Mice's erratic leader, had slashed off an employee's ear and screamed through the loudspeakers that consumerism was dead—*the Blind Mice were bringing deliverance to all, free of charge!*—while Durwood sneaked up from behind in an invisibility suit.

Now, I watched Kent Kirkland exit Shop-All and push a shopping cart up the CZ-7 aisle to the trunk of his sedan. I squinted over my steering wheel to see his haul.

Toilet paper, thirty-six-roll economy pack.

Several boxes of Fiber One cereal.

Produce. Apples and broccoli.

My eyelids drifted closed. When they popped back open, I thought, *Things have to change*.

I'd chased down Martha Dodson's hunch. I'd stuck with it longer than I should have to validate her in her husband's eyes. But Kent Kirkland wasn't holding two boys hostage. He was looking out for his colorectal health.

I gave up the tail and drove home. I would call Martha and tell her I believed she was a smart, compassionate person and a keen observer, but mistaken in this.

First, though, I needed a plan. Abandoning this case would create a hole in my schedule—and my bank account. I'd been stiffed by the client before Martha, the husband of a cheating wife who turned out *not* to be cheating, and I couldn't afford too long a gap in income. I should be squirreling away money for Zach's college, and neither of my exes paid child support.

At home, I checked my McGill Investigators inbox. I had a backlog of potential cases, messages I needed to respond to. I could run background on the "worthless, pierced-up boyfriend" of a teen daughter in Rockaway. I could insert myself into a homeowners' association dispute about chartreuse, which may or may not have been removed from the New Vernon HOA list of approved pastels in retaliation for a dog's barking.

The least-bad option was probably Alec Blackburn. He wanted me to dig into a small but very profitable investment firm before accepting their job offer. Detailed financial analysis wasn't my forte, but Alec's message had sounded respectful, non-crazy.

Also: "Alec Blackburn." *Imagine the jawline.*

Honestly, the smartest move might've been putting my

PI business on hiatus and calling Rainey Personnel instead. Temp work paid better on a per-hour basis. A lot of Rainey's jobs were brainless paperwork, copy-collate stuff, but maybe I would luck out with a reception gig. At least with those you got to meet new people.

I was just weighing options, the stapler versus the jawline, when my doorbell rang.

I peeked around the living room curtains. Standing on my porch, palming his neck, was Detective Art Judd.

A jolt passed through me—of excitement, of fear, of hope? I wasn't sure.

Karen came halfway down the stairs.

"I'll get it," I said from the door. "It looks like somebody from one of my cases."

She clutched Blue Elephant, excitedly crushing his well-worn trunk. "Is it a lying husband?"

"No," I said. "Not a husband."

"Is it a creepy neighbor? A creepy neighbor hiding a *big* secret?"

I shook my head. "Not creepy. No secret."

Disappointed, she turned back upstairs with Blue Elephant.

I checked my hair in the hallway mirror—a little frizzy but at least symmetrical—and answered the door.

Art Judd ducked his head. "Sorry to intrude, Miss McGill. But I have some information for you."

"Information?" I said. "About Calvin Witt and Jhonny Ramos?"

"Yes. Well, about Jhonny."

I peered past him to the street, where he'd parked. "Do you generally make house calls?"

"I don't, no." He fingered the cuffs of his shirt, which

looked new or at least newly pressed. "You, uh, made an impression."

I felt that jolt again—deep inside, warmer.

It must've shown through because Art Judd continued, sheepish, "You had so much passion for Martha. For those boys. And the truth is, hey, we haven't had much luck. The trail's gone cold on them both."

"But you think one's in Venezuela and the other's..."

He nodded. "I do, but you never know. Can't hurt to have another pair of boots on the ground."

I looked at my feet automatically. They were in socks, white with purple pom-poms at the heels.

Art Judd followed my look down. "It's what we say, 'boots on the ground.' Just an expression."

"Sure," I said, my toes curling under.

Our eyes danced, not quite meeting but not looking away either. I was vaguely aware that I had a question to ask, an important question, but I kept blanking out on what it was.

He pointed to the porch swing, where Hedgie Hedgehog and Frogger sat side by side.

"I see you've got children," he said. "How old?"

"Six and fourteen," I said.

He smiled as though remembering the ages fondly. "My daughter's sixteen. Little different story."

"How so?"

His smile broadened. He hadn't given many smiles at the police station two weeks ago. This one was nice—generous, slightly crooked under the mustache.

"When they're sixteen," he said, "they know more than you."

"I get that. Zach took a personal finance elective—now

he's telling me I should be investing in alternative energy stocks."

"Yeah, but at sixteen they're right." Art Judd chuckled, his eyes inward. "My Crystal, she really does. She knows. I can't help her with trigonometry. Or boys."

I gave him a moment to finish the thought in his head. "Your wife might do better on the boy topic."

His brow furrowed in confusion. Then, with a start, he looked at the ring on his left hand.

"We're divorced—I should take this thing off," he said. "But I doubt my ex does any better than me. Crystal's a handful."

"They..." I began. "Your ex-wife has custody?"

He nodded. "I get every other weekend. It's best. Being a detective, you can't be the primary. I was around a lot, before. But you get jerked around."

"Is that why it—er, didn't work?"

The question was out before I registered how nosy it sounded.

But Art Judd was grinning. "Nope. It didn't work because my wife slept with her twenty-three-year-old trainer."

"Ah."

I watched for signs of psychological damage. The detective's eyes did have a glassy quality, but there was strength in his chin. Resolve.

"Those were exactly my thoughts," he said. "'Ah.'"

I tried for a lighthearted shrug. "At least your daughter should be on your side, right?"

"Nah." He shook his head. "We didn't tell her about the trainer, and of course he was out the door in nothing flat. We blamed my work."

I felt my back teeth gritting. "That's awful. Why?"

"She's living with her mother. Her and her mother, that's the important thing." Art Judd's mouth quivered, then set. "It's better this way. For everybody."

Except you, I thought, my heart bubbling up.

My own divorce from Zach's father had been 180-degrees different. Not only had Rick been the one to cheat —he'd managed to blame the affair on me. Because I'd turned naggy. Because I hadn't kept things "exciting enough." (Coming from a man whose own bedroom repertoire was about as varied as grab-'n'-go breakfast options from a gas station.) All throughout the ordeal, he'd made himself the victim, no matter that I'd never laid a finger on another man, was logging thirty hours a week with Rainey Personnel, *and* continued to breastfeed Zach.

I took a new look at Art Judd. This large, capable man standing on my porch. Resigned. Regretful. I saw details I'd missed before—a gray hair at the temple, rosy roundness in his cheeks. I couldn't believe he'd just shown up here today. I couldn't believe what he'd told me about Crystal. "*My* Crystal." His brown eyes seemed to have another level, as though the pupils were sitting in tiny flowing meadows.

I rushed to kiss him.

Surprise in his lips quickly yielded, and his eyes closed. The moment was sudden and bright. I hardly knew what I was doing, he surely felt ambushed—but we turned off our brains and gave in. Our fingertips touched.

The screen door wheezed open, interrupting.

"My, my."

I separated my lips reluctantly from Art's. Granny stood in the doorway.

"I didn't realize you were expecting a gentleman caller," she said.

"No, Granny," I said, "I wasn't expecting. This just..."

The septuagenarian's eyes sank impossibly deeper into their sockets as she waited for the rest of my sentence.

The detective took my hand and said, "Happened."

"Yes, it just happened," I recovered. "Do you need me for something?"

Granny ignored the question, scrutinizing my visitor instead. In the manner of seniors, she didn't bother disguising her intentions. She gaped openly at his face, his shirt, his hands—which, I noticed now, were hairy.

"Swarthy," she said.

"Grandmother! Can you please—"

"That means what I think it means, doesn't it?" she said, looking at Art. "Dark and hairy like?"

He said, "I believe that is the definition, ma'am."

Feeling a hard buzz all through my body, I said through clenched teeth, *"Do you need me for something?"*

Granny continued to inspect the detective. "Aw, he's fine. Tell you what, I prefer him to that cad Rafferty. Now you don't consort with prostitutes, do you?"

"He's a detective, Grandmother."

"That's no guarantee. No, sir, there's dirty detectives." She looked at him, sidelong. "Are ya, dirty? Do you take advantage of the prostitutes when you book them?"

"Enough—that's enough," I said. "Now, once more, is there something I can help you with? Did the cable go out again? Are you having trouble finding a Tupperware lid?"

She looked lost for a moment, squinting. Then she opened her mouth and jerked toward me. Then she was lost again.

Finally, she said, "The bra load! Where's the bra load? You did them separate, didn't you?"

As I struggled to hide my mortification, she looked to Art, who'd become suddenly interested in the porch bricks.

"I apologize, I'm taking my time getting ready today," Granny said, wriggling her torso by way of explanation.

The detective's face took on a green tint. He shuffled in place, then, seeming to remember something, he perked up and found a scrap of paper in his pocket.

"Becky Ramos—Jhonny's mom," he said, handing me the scrap. "I forgot to put down the area code, but it's 908."

Our fingers brushed as I accepted the paper.

He hiked his thumb back toward the street. "I, uh, gotta get back to the station. If you call Becky, don't say where you got her number. They could take my badge."

Granny pointed to the paper. "See! That's dirty, just like I predicted. I told you he might be dirty."

I faced Art feeling a fresh wave of mortification, but he seemed to absorb it somehow with those soft eyes, in that bristling mustache.

I mouthed, *Thank you.*

He mouthed back, *We'll talk.*

Granny's narrowed eyes zipped between us. "What? What is it?"

"Nothing, Granny." I draped my arm across her shoulders and headed us inside. "Now let's see if we can't find that missing load of laundry."

CHAPTER TEN

After getting Granny squared away with undergarments, I walked Art's scrap of paper to the dining room—the quietest in the house—to call Becky Ramos. My head was still swirling from the kiss, but I couldn't spare the brain cycles to interpret it now, to wonder where Art Judd fit in my life, to question whether my wildly premature move had been a stroke of madness, or genius, or some misguided reaction to Quaid Rafferty, or what.

I needed to focus on the case. I needed to figure out if it was dead like I'd thought twenty minutes ago, or if Jhonny's mother had information that changed the equation.

I tapped Becky's number into my phone.

"Mom, when're you making lunch?" Zach shouted. "What happened to you? I'm hungry."

Seconds later, he tracked me down and stood at the door with a strained expression. I half expected him to open his beak so I could feed him my own regurgitated food.

"You're fourteen years old," I said. "Is it possible you could address that need yourself?"

He raised a shoulder. "I mean, I could open a bag of mint Oreos."

"Address it in a *healthful* and *time-of-day-appropriate* manner?"

Karen preempted his response, calling from the kitchen, "Mommy, can I have a snack?"

I cleared Becky Ramos's number and put away my phone. One kiddo crying hunger might be a fluke, but two means you've flubbed your meal scheduling. Between my spontaneous kiss and the promise of a new lead, I'd forgotten lunch.

In the kitchen, Karen was nosing around a four-pack of lemon puddings.

"No, honey," I said. "It's lunchtime. I'll make you some lunch."

"But I want a snack!" She thrust her lower lip forward.

"We're eating lunch." I replaced the puddings on their shelf and opened the fridge, unfurling one arm like a game-show attendant. "I have leftover stew. I have honey-glazed turkey for sandwiches..."

I paused, awaiting enthusiasm. Karen's eyes stayed longingly on the puddings.

I continued, "There's tuna, there's refried beans for a burrito..."

She screwed up her eyes and frowned.

I looked at the microwave clock. I really wanted to make my phone call, to figure out whether I had a live case going or needed to get in touch with Rainey Personnel.

"Or," I said, defeat heavy in my voice, "I could make a box of mac 'n' chee—"

"Mac 'n' cheese, mac 'n' cheese!" Karen clapped and hopped in place. "Thank you, Mommy!"

I set a pot of water to boil, lopped off a finger of butter, and dumped in the contents of that thin, blue, magical box. As I waited for the macaroni to soften, I considered Becky Ramos. With no son to cook for. Abandoned by her husband. How had she gotten through? How did she face each new day without curling into a ball on her mattress and sobbing?

Maybe she did. I'd read online that she had grown up in Utah and moved here for her husband's job. Did she think about moving back home? Living with her parents or extended family?

Zach's voice: "Is it *done* yet?"

Then Karen: "Can I play phone, Mommy?"

"Just about," I called to Zach, and slid my phone to Karen.

"Ugh, I've been waiting *forever*," Zach whined.

I felt a flash of anger. Maybe because I'd been thinking of Becky's tragedy, or because I was hungry myself, or tired —I don't know, the complaint irked me. Where did these entitled reactions come from? We weren't rich. Not by a long shot. I had tried to instill perspective in Zach, to show thankfulness for this nice home (which I could barely afford) and the good health of our family. I'd tried not to coddle him.

Maybe I did, though. Maybe I subconsciously compensated for the absence of his father. Maybe I tolerated too much.

"We're going to get more serious about chores," I said, setting the colander in the sink. "I remember you were going to be on trash takeout first and third weeks." I confirmed the dates on our Catspirations wall calendar. "How's that going?"

Both our gazes went to the kitchen trash. The lid sat crooked, a crumpled pizza box poking out.

Zach pointed upstairs. "I'm gonna, um, get my algebra homework. I'll do some while I eat."

I told him that sounded fine, happy to take schoolwork however I could get it.

Seven minutes later, I drained the macaroni, dumped in the cheese powder, and added my secret ingredient: a teaspoon of Dijon mustard. Then I divvied out the gooey goodness about sixty-Zach and forty-Karen. I would eat after from whatever they left on their plates.

Karen tried forking up hers one-handed while playing SparklePopper on my phone.

"We're eating, honey," I said, gently taking back the phone. "Let's sit together and enjoy each other's company."

I smiled, squaring my shoulders to her.

"But I hafta finish my level!" she said. "I was almost to the next level."

I shook my head. I'd learned my lesson with levels. They were either so hard they took forever, or so easy you finished fast and just had to start the next one.

"Later this afternoon, once you've done your good reading," I said, "it's possible we'll find a minute or two for SparklePopper."

Karen took a shifty look at the phone like she was thinking about swiping it anyway.

"*Okay*," she grumped.

With electronics out of the way, Karen's portion disappeared quickly from her plate. So did Zach's. I stole furtive glances at his homework. It looked like he solved two problems out of a worksheet numbered to ten—not rock-star pace, but solid enough progress.

I oversaw their rinsing and loading of plates into the dishwasher, filled the mac 'n' cheesy pot with soapy water, and returned to the dining room to call Becky Ramos.

I didn't reach her on the first try, or the second ten minutes later. Finally, at quarter past one, I got an answer.

"Who's this?" said an out-of-breath voice.

"Molly McGill," I said. "I'm investigating missing boys in this vicinity, and I was told—"

"Venezuela," the voice interrupted. "My son was kidnapped to Venezuela. I'm surprised you need to harass a grieving mother to find that out."

Over the line, I heard background chatter and the tones of a cash register.

"I apologize," I said. "Yes, I'm aware that your husband, your ex-husband, has been accused of taking Jhonny."

"Accused? What are you implying?"

I lowered the phone from my ear. The interview was off to a bad start, clearly. I'd assumed Becky Ramos would be receptive based on my mission—to find her son—but she must be inundated with media calls digging for a scoop. I needed to flip the script, to put myself on her side.

"I believe Jhonny may still be in New Jersey," I said.

"You believe? Do you have—" She broke off to say something away from the phone, then resumed, "Do you have some information, some inside dirt? Or are you just torturing me?"

I took a measured breath. "I'm not saying one hundred percent. I'm sure you've been through the ringer with false hopes, and conspiracy theories, and your heart probably breaks every time. I...I'd just like to talk."

Leaving out names and locations, I laid out the reason for my call: I was tracking a suspicious individual who my client feared was holding one or more boys hostage. The timeline fit her son's disappearance. All I wanted was a moment of her time to hear about Jhonny and the circumstances surrounding his case.

Becky—who was finishing up her shift at Dollar General—gave me her address and said to meet her there in half an hour. I asked Granny to keep an eye on the kids and headed out.

Becky's apartment complex had a cruddy parking lot. I prayed for my car's skinny tires as we bumped over gravel and potholes and tufts of weeds. I peered past abandoned bikes and whiffle bats for Becky's unit number. The one I thought was hers had window air-conditioning and a plywood door.

I parked and started hesitantly up the walk. I heard crying inside, then shrieking.

Before I could form any theories, a boxy car zipped into the spot beside mine.

"Hey, we about tied," said the curly-haired driver. "You're Molly McGill?"

She hustled alongside me still in her work uniform, black with a yellow name tag. She grinned wearily at the door. "Let's see what the damage looks like, huh?"

The crying intensified when we entered, like train noise your first step outside to the platform. A babysitter who couldn't have been older than thirteen was already in her coat. She held out her palm, took Becky's twenty-dollar bill, and left.

Becky hoisted one toddler—the source of the crying—

up from a wheeled walker. The other, a carbon copy, looked on holding a squished juice box.

"How was your"—Becky faltered getting a grip on the child—"day, girls?"

They erupted with a string of *me-me* and *na-na* and *mmph-mmphs*. The second girl wanted to be picked up now too. As Becky bent to scoop her, the juice box ended up dribbling blue down her arm.

"Twins," I said, feeling slightly shell-shocked.

"You betcha," she said. "Double trouble."

Eventually they squirmed down. One tottered into the kitchenette area and found a New-Age-y crystal to pick up, drawing Becky. The other headed for the stairs.

"Oh, let's keep away from those," I said with a tastes-like-asparagus face.

The girl kept coming so I picked up a stray Nerf ball and, waving it through her sight line, bounced it enticingly. The girls' eyes spun in place. She grabbed for it.

When Becky reappeared from the kitchenette, I thought of recommending a baby gate but decided against.

I have friends who would turn and run screaming from the chaos here. It actually brought a smile to my lips, though. A tired, grateful smile. I'd been here in the corralling stage, hanging on for dear life, not putting the toys away perfectly because they'll just be pulled out five minutes later. Becky had a system, I could see. Books and board games on the left side of the room, balls and stuffed animals on the right.

Mostly.

"So you had your twins with Jhonny, before he was taken?" I said, guessing at ages and doing the math.

"Yeah, it was nuts," Becky said. "And Esteban was

checked out. He'd already decided to go home to Venezuela —I'm sure of that."

She described the twins' madcap first year, teething, blocked milk ducts, all while Jhonny was having his own struggles in fourth grade. Apparently his classmates had caught on that he couldn't read yet.

"They told him his parents couldn't even spell 'Johnny' right," she said. "That must be why he turned out stupid."

My heart twisted. "Sometimes kids are awful."

Becky sighed in agreement.

I said, "I suppose Esteban wasn't much help?"

"He helped some with Jhonny. He had an interest in Jhonny, unlike the girls, who just made him mad." She leaned closer confidentially. "It's part of the culture, to favor boys. I think it's why the family decided to kidnap Jhonny."

As her daughters spun around the apartment, my heart kept twisting.

"There's too much of that in the world, I'm afraid."

The girls fell into each other like bowling pins. Then they rolled over and struggled back up.

Becky said, "But Esteban, he had his moments. He cooked. He could sing like an angel."

"Was that his profession? A musician?"

"No, his family would've never gone for that. They paid for his MBA. He was going into finance, or else get cut out of the fortune."

I said nothing, but Becky obviously sensed my disapproval.

"Growing up in that clan—it was so much pressure," she explained. "And like I said, he had his good points. He did stuff. He found that great tutoring center for Jhonny. You know that place downtown, We Will Rise!"

I said I did. We Will Rise! was a fantastic story, started several years ago by a man named Andre Wilcox who'd grown up in the Morristown slums and gone on to be an aerospace executive. In retirement, he'd established the center as a place where at-risk youth could hang out and receive guidance.

"Jhonny loved it there," Becky said. "They put him with good tutors, and he made progress. His reading didn't get quite to grade level, but it was coming."

She gazed at a framed school picture on the wall, beside an astrology chart, of Jhonny in a bolo tie. I had only seen his image on my computer screen until now. In this larger view, Jhonny's smile reached for his earlobes. His eyes glimmered like he was holding in a laugh—maybe a class-mate had been goofing off behind the photographer.

I said, "I'm sorry."

Becky smiled off a weakness in her cheeks. "That was the last place anybody saw him—the center. Esteban and his family took him that night."

"Straight from We Will Rise!?"

Becky nodded. "They—they didn't let him say goodbye. Or take his Ironman toothbrush." Now the weakness became a quivering. Tears started down her face. I stepped forward into a hug.

The twins were watching as their mother sobbed at my shoulder. I made myself smile at them. On my mental list of things to ask, there was one biggie I hadn't gotten to: Why hadn't Becky put herself on a plane to Venezuela, marched into Esteban's parents' house—or palace, or compound—and demanded back her son? The question had bothered me since the moment Art had described Jhonny's situation.

Now, though, looking into her daughters' faces, despair

pulsing through our joined bodies, I understood. Becky Ramos felt powerless. The world had put a sheer cliff in front of her. She could climb it if she chose, battle her wealthy in-laws on their turf, forfeit a week's pay at Dollar General plus whatever the plane ticket cost. Almost certainly she'd lose and be stuck in even worse straits with her girls, the only worthwhile thing left in her life. The only fight she could still win.

A noise sounded outside. Heavy and hydraulic, some truck.

The girl who'd had the juice box earlier said, "Cycle, cycle!"

Then the other's eyes lit up too. "Cycle, Momma, *cycle!*"

Becky broke free of me and, sniffing her eyes clear, rushed to the kitchen.

"Okay, I hear you two, let's get the recycling out," she said, and handed them each a small handled container with empty cans and flattened Lucky Charms boxes. She carried a bigger container herself.

I froze. As they hustled for the front door, I was staring at Becky's container—the bigger one.

It was clear.

Inside, at the bottom-right corner, was a crumpled gold-and-green wrapper. A granola bar wrapper.

Bright Ones.

CHAPTER ELEVEN

I didn't tell Becky Ramos about the bars in Kent Kirkland's pantry. I wanted to—lurching toward the recycling container, feeling my eyes bug out. Then I remembered I wasn't giving names or locations.

"What?" Becky said, noticing my reaction. "You're looking at the take-out dishes, right? I know they're supposed to be totally free of food or else it messes up the sorting machines, but—"

"No, I...it's just that brand," I said. "Bright Ones. I've never tried them."

She peeked out the window, confirming the truck had a few units to go before hers.

"I don't love them myself," she said. "I just had some around. They were Jhonny's favorite."

I controlled my eyes, which wanted to bug even wider. I thanked her for her time and promised to be in touch with any developments pertaining to her son.

The twins waved goodbye from the plywood door.

On the drive home, my thoughts were on fire. Now I

had a direct link from Kirkland to one of Martha's proposed victims. Jhonny wasn't just some name Martha had connected from a newspaper to her odd neighbor. I'd met his mother and sisters. I'd seen his school picture. I'd learned what kind of granola bar he ate, the same kind Kent Kirkland appeared to keep on hand.

The case had gotten serious. I thought about what needed to happen, investigation-wise. This wasn't a lark anymore. There was a real possibility those boys were in Kirkland's house.

What's the quickest way to get inside for a search?

Stopped for a light at the intersection of Vine and DeBussy Road, I came to a difficult decision: it was time to bring in the professionals. I believed in myself and my abilities, but there were limits to what I could do. I couldn't obtain a warrant from a judge. I couldn't force my way into Kirkland's home and claim probably cause afterward. Not legally.

And Kirkland would never, ever let me back in voluntarily.

I called Art Judd from my driveway, not wanting to risk going inside and finding the dining room phone booth occupied.

"Hi, Art?" I said. "It's Molly McGill. I was hoping we could talk."

"Uh, s-sure," he said, possibly in the middle of something. "How about over dinner?"

Then I remembered our exchange on the porch, him mouthing, *We'll talk.*

He thought this was about, well, us.

"Dinner would be fine," I said. "I mean, dinner would be great. Of course."

I thought I caught a relieved sigh. Then he said, "There's this sushi joint, Pi's Sushi. It's halfway between here and Morristown. Whaddaya say?"

Sushi was an unexpected choice. Somehow I'd thought he would suggest Maggiano's or some bar and grill, but I said absolutely. We agreed to meet at six. I'd been hoping to talk immediately and get the ball rolling for Jhonny (and Calvin?), but this was okay. It gave me time to read with Karen and make myself presentable.

Reading was terrific—Karen battled through two Fancy Nancy books herself, then listened to me read sixty pages of *Judy Moody Girl Detective*. Zach even got drawn in, lingering by the front door with his skateboard in his armpit, smirking along with the lines from Judy's brother, Stink.

At 5:15, I found my eyeliner pen and a decent tube of lipstick.

"Are you seeing the dirty cop?" Granny asked, invading my bathroom.

I popped my lips, deciding how I liked the shade. "I am meeting Detective Judd, yes."

She rubbed her hands cantankerously. "You gonna wear a wire?"

"Why would I do that?"

"In case he tries something." Granny drew back her seamed face, holding the halves of her robe together at the neck. "Then you'll have proof, dead to rights."

She watches a lot of daytime judge shows, which gives her this DIY perspective on justice. Last year, she'd suggested to Zach that he "serve papers" on a teacher who'd marked him down unfairly. When pressed, she had no idea what sort of papers or how Zach might go about serving them.

(Likewise, Zach had no explanation for the unfair grade except, "Reggie got full credit and he wrote down, like, basically the same thing.")

I wiped off the lipstick and reapplied lighter. "I think I'll risk it and go surveillance free."

"Pshaw." She shook her head piteously. "You always were naive."

I finished up at the vanity and slipped into a sensible dress. Downstairs, I set a box of spaghetti on the range.

Zach said, "Pasta again?"

I added a jar of tomato sauce. "Unless you were planning to make duck à l'orange. Remind Granny to do a veg too, okay?"

He said he would.

"And cranberry sauce is not a veg," I warned.

I found my keys, purse, jacket. My cell phone wasn't where I normally kept it beside the toaster. I hunted around a bit before hearing a familiar sequence of *pips* and *bings* from the dining room.

"Karen," I called, and discovered her bent in the corner over a color-glowing screen.

"I'm almost done!" she protested. "Just one more red diamond, one more..."

I crossed the room and pried my phone away. The sound Karen made—keening, desperate—conjured up nagging anxieties about how she was growing up, all these technology crutches. I'd been trying to set an example by using my phone minimally, keeping the charger on the nightstand and limiting myself to a single overnight charge per day.

Sometimes this came back to bite me, like now. My battery was at 4 percent.

"How long have you been playing?" I asked.

The six-year-old gulped.

I said, "We're going to have a constructive talk when I get home." Then I reached deep for a warm smile and kissed her forehead. "Have fun with Granny and your brother. And Hedgie Hedgehog."

Pi's Sushi had a dismal location—the end storefront of a mostly vacant strip mall—but a nifty sign with bubbling neon fish. Art Judd was waiting for me at the first table, wearing a dress shirt and loosened tie. I waved to him through the window.

"Cute place," I said. "I guess you've eaten here before?"

"My daughter introduced me." The detective raised a pair of chopsticks, which looked like toothpicks between his broad fingers. "It's not a lot of bang for your buck, the portions. But it tastes right."

A server brought us hot tea and menus. As I scanned the options, I was aware of my feet sharing space with Art Judd's, shifting, fitting around the table legs.

He seemed to know his order already, being a regular, and sat watching me.

"Your kids ever try sushi?" he asked.

"Once, in Trenton," I said. "They did alright. Karen was creeped out by the whole raw thing, but she ate the California and cucumber rolls."

Art drummed the table with his thumb. "Zach?"

I was impressed he'd remembered the name. "Him too. Of course, first he asked if they served blowfish. You know that special fish—it's poisonous, it has to be prepared just so or else it kills you?"

"Sounds familiar. That's not some urban legend?"

I puffed my cheeks. "Who knows. This place didn't have

it. But Zach ate everything they brought out. I'm not sure he had a real complex appreciation. I asked them afterward which was their favorite roll, and he said, 'The rice one.'"

Art laughed. "I get where he's coming from. By the time I'm done dunking mine in the soy sauce and that spicy green stuff? Hey, it all eats pretty nice."

We shared a comfortable look. I was here on business, but the nonbusiness end of things was feeling hopeful. I wondered what kind of rapport he might have with Zach. I liked this lighthearted side of him.

Before my thoughts got too beamy, I stopped myself.

Slow it down, McGill.

These were some pretty thin bones for the kind of soup I was lusting after—one kiss and an unexpectedly enlightened restaurant choice.

"No brothers or sisters for Crystal?" I asked.

"Nope," he said. "She was plenty."

He grinned, but it seemed forced. Did he regret not having a bigger, happier family? Did he wish for a son to play catch with? (Wishing for one to do ollies with at the skate park would be asking too much.)

"I suppose it's been an adjustment," I said. "Only getting those weekends with her."

The forced grin went flat. Art fiddled with the empty wrapper his chopsticks had come in.

"Eh, it breaks your heart. Every night, you walk into a kitchen with no backpack, nobody rolling their eyes and saying you need a car with better gas mileage."

"Crystal was an environmentalist?"

Art set down his chopsticks in parallel lines. "She is, yeah."

The change from past to present tense was gentle, but I

caught it and felt bad. My own divorces had been rotten and grueling and—in those transitional months—full of anguish. But Zach and Karen had been my anchors, my constant reminders to keep putting one foot in front of the other. I couldn't imagine surviving without them.

"I'm sure she misses those nights too," I said.

The tables here were tiny, leaving Art's hands few places to go. It was cute watching them fidget, fitting behind the ornate kettle, idly picking up an appetizer plate—like a wafer in his large hands. Now, our eyes meeting, one reached out to hold three of my fingers.

We sipped cloudy miso soup and sucked the salt off half a plate of edamame. Art was a wonderful listener. For several minutes as I spoke, his mouth never closed all the way, staying open in a morphing expression of surprise, agreement, and fascination. Once, I lost my train of thought watching this—watching him watching me.

He's probably just used to flattering people, I told myself. *All those witness interviews.*

But I didn't quite believe this. I believed that he was good.

Dinner was going so well that I almost hated to bring up Jhonny Ramos. I had this small whispering worry that moving away from shared topics of conversation—children, weeknight cooking, whether to root for the Eagles or Giants —to one in which Art was the authority risked upsetting the balance.

Still, it had to be done. I couldn't let date dynamics stand in the way of possibly recovering Jhonny.

"So I did pay a visit to Becky Ramos," I said. "Thanks again for giving me her information."

He ducked his head and finished chewing a bite of

yellowtail. "No problem. How is Becky? I recall she had her hands full at home."

"Yes, she still does," I said. "But she's making it work."

"Good, she deserves some luck. I wish like hell we could've got the State Department, somebody, to help with Venezuela."

I took a while preparing the roll on my plate, tapping it to the center, adding a dot of wasabi.

"Right," I said. "Actually, I noticed something at her apartment—something that made me think Jhonny could be here."

Art's brow crimped. He glanced toward the next table, then at the register.

I said, "In New Jersey."

"You're talking about Kent Kirkland?"

"Yes," I said. "I was thinking the department might want to take a closer look at him."

The detective tried controlling his face but couldn't stop a slight wince. His eyes lost some of their life.

"Hm," he said. "That's, uh, interesting. What did you find out?"

My chest was pounding, his skepticism like a black veil between us. I made myself keep going.

"A granola bar wrapper," I said, and explained the match between Brenda's recycling and the box in Kirkland's pantry.

Art's barrel chest rose and fell in a breath. "What's this brand, Bright One?"

"Bright *Ones*," I said. "As in, 'Feed these to your kids, they'll make her bright.'"

He nodded. Then he tapped the table. Then he nodded again.

"Lotta people eat granola bars nowadays," he said.

"I'm aware of that."

"Some of 'em, you know, it's like candy. With the choco-late and caramel and—"

"Yes, you have to read the nutritional labels carefully." My jaw clenched. "Trust me on this. Bright Ones bars are tiny. They're quite clearly a children's product, and Kent Kirkland is a grown man. A grown and supposedly child-less man."

Art's top lip folded under his bottom. "I understand that."

"I don't think you do." *Cool it, Molly,* I thought, but couldn't keep an edge from my voice. "They were also Jhonny Ramos's favorite kind. Not Nutri-Grain, not Kind bars, not Clif or Quaker or Kashi. Jhonny liked Bright Ones —and now a very odd, very suspicious man who lives in the general vicinity of his disappearance has a box of them in his house."

"Mm," Art said. "Kidnapper who buys his victims their favorite foods."

"He isn't so much cruel as controlling." I realized I was speculating badly, stepping out on a limb. "It fits his psych profile."

"Look, I know you've got specialized training. But saying this Kirkland guy's odd or suspicious, that's up for interpreta—"

"Scratch that, fine." I snapped my arms closed. "He's normal. It's totally normal to hack up every flower in your mailbox planter in a bloodthirsty fit."

The restaurant wasn't busy, and a few heads had turned our way. The server—who also worked the register—sounded extra cheery ringing up a customer.

Art palmed his chin.

"I'm being respectful as I can, Molly." He said my name with a plea in the middle. "Granola bars...what this Kirkland did or didn't have in his pantry...it's a clue. A reason to keep plugging on your side, maybe. But it doesn't rise to the level of us making a move."

My face burned. "Bright Ones is not a common brand."

"I understand."

"You keep saying that, 'I understand.'"

"Listen, ninety-five percent of missing children are runaways. Of the few that aren't, ninety-nine-point-nine percent get taken by family members." Art turned his palms up. "Now, math's not my strong suit. But those odds are awful long."

"Every case is unique," I said. "Jhonny's unique. Kent Kirkland is beyond unique."

Art pulled one shoe up to the opposite knee. "These kidnapper types have a record, generally. It's rare we see one without a violent past arrest."

Then he sat looking at me. It annoyed me that he didn't just finish his point, that he made me ask. "I suppose you pulled his record?"

Art nodded. "Couldn't even scrounge up a parking ticket."

Furthermore, he'd tracked down Kent Kirkland's boss in Seattle—Kirkland worked remotely—who described her employee of seven years as "diligent," "reliable," and "regimented."

"She said he could be prickly on certain things," Art recounted. "He didn't like meetings during 'the dinner hour.' But he finished assignments well and on time."

"*Dinner hour*," I muttered. "Did he ever fly off the handle?"

"Not that she told me. Kirkland sounds like, you know, a down-the-middle worker bee."

I looked around at the plates, rectangular with fluted edges and Japanese characters.

"There could be things in his juvenile record," I said, groping. "Things you can't see."

"There could," Art said. "That's why I talked to his old teachers. He attended Jefferson Heights, across town. They said he was unremarkable. Had truancy problems in elementary, but clean as a whistle once he hit high school."

The truancy was strange. Of course, truancy in elementary school is more about parents than children. Karen was guaranteed to spill something and reject four pairs of pants every morning; it was on me to work around these minor crises and get her to class before the tardy bell.

"I still think," I said, "you need eyes inside that house. Inside Kent Kirkland's basement."

He inhaled through his nose, clearly losing patience.

"We conduct investigations based on hard evidence—that's how we do it. Eyewitness accounts. Fingerprints." He counted on his thumb. "If we chased every oddball connection, we'd—"

"Oddball?"

"—we'd burn through our manpower in nothing flat. You just can't run a department that way."

He was looking at me plaintively, his hand spread flat between us in an appeal for reason.

"I certainly wouldn't want your precious manpower burned," I said.

"Molly."

"What? Why did you give me Becky Ramos's number anyway? If you were just going to ignore what I found."

He looked suddenly dyspeptic, shifting in his chair. "Wh— I, well, I knew you wanted the mother's phone number, so I..."

"Humored me?" I said. "Used it as an excuse to show up on my front porch?"

I was flushed, breathing darts.

Art stared down at the table where not long ago he'd held my fingers.

"The granola bars, I'll give you—it is a connection. It could be significant. But I'd have to see more in order to devote resources."

"Okay," I said, seizing the opening. "Okay, that's good because I have another lead. We Will Rise!, that tutoring center downtown? Jhonny was there the night he disappeared."

"We know that."

"And you've interviewed all the employees there? And any kids who knew Jhonny?"

"A significant number, yes."

"Well, I'm going to interview some more," I said. "I'm going to drive down tonight and look for more connections. Look for that 'hard' evidence." I hate air quotes, but I did them now anyway.

"That's a rough part of town," the detective said.

"It's not that bad."

"Molly, homicide statistics are my business, and I can tell you—"

"Don't," I interrupted, grinning tightly. "Alright? Please don't. Please don't tell me."

The rest of dinner was predictably terrible. Dropping the

topic of Kirkland, we had perfunctory discussions of the school spring break calendar and roadwork on the New Jersey Turnpike. I ate most of the shrimp and avocado rolls. He favored spicy tuna. At the end, a single piece was left between us, standing up like a coin stuck between heads and tails.

"You go 'head," Art said, gesturing with his chopstick."

"No, you," I said. "I'm full."

Neither of us ate it.

We split the bill and gathered our jackets.

Outside, the sun had set. The strip mall's only other tenant, a vaping smoke shop, had closed. Its shopkeeper was raising blinds and flapping a rug to help the noxious fumes escape. The parking lot felt chilly and empty. I side-stepped grease pools, streaked with murky colors by the neon light of the Pi's Sushi sign.

Art split off for his car. "Thanks for driving out here."

"No problem," I said. "Thank you, it was good to...to talk."

He joined his hands over his belt buckle. "I wish you wouldn't go down to that place, We Will Rise! Not by yourself."

I let an angry reflex pass before answering.

"I am going," I said. "Jhonny spent a lot of time there."

"That neighborhood gets dangerous."

"I've faced danger. Plenty."

Art smiled, tossing his keys idly in his hand. "With those Third Chance guys? Quaid and, what, Durwood?"

So he'd done his homework.

"That's right," I said. "I was in the Blind Mice. What were you guys doing during the Anarchy, down at the police station?"

He squinted into the distance. "Hiding under our desks, mostly." His eyes came back to me. "I still don't want you to go."

I pursed my lips—*fair enough*—and extended my hand for a shake. When Art took it, I felt the disappointment in his touch like damp laundry in the dryer: a whole hour tumbling around for nothing.

CHAPTER TWELVE

I drove home. I was pleased to find Granny had more or less succeeded with dinner. The pasta had been prepared and eaten, all but a few strands at the bottom of the pot, and she'd served the tart-cherry-vinaigrette salad kit for veg. She had missed the kit's baggie of croutons—I found it wedged deep in the corner of the larger bag—but I wasn't about to deduct points there.

"Thank you, Granny," I said, dropping my keys on the counter.

Granny was dividing a package of Skittles with Karen for dessert. She had an incorrigible sweet tooth.

"Thought I'd burn down the house, did ya?" she said. "I know how to cook. Cooked for all my brothers and sisters during the Depression."

I nodded, containerizing the leftover salad. She'd been born in 1938, actually.

Zach ambled in from the living room. "How'd your date go?"

"It wasn't a date," I said. "I met up with a detective as part of the Dodson case."

Granny called, "The swarthy one?"

Zach snorted.

Karen stopped twisting her hair through a scrunchie to ask what "swarthy" meant.

"It's not important, honey," I said, "because this was not a date."

I didn't like how that came out, and thought about explaining that swarthiness—or any purely physical attribute—shouldn't determine a person's appeal. But that would just undermine my denial.

Granny was holding a Skittle up to the light. She preferred reds. "Better make sure he's not dirty before you go making him husband numero three."

"Art Judd is an upstanding, non-dirty detective," I said. *And not on track to be husband numero anything.*

She popped the Skittle—orange, as it turned out—into her mouth. Then she squinted ominously.

"A cop is never what he seems," she declared. "They're trained for it—they're trained to deceive! You only see the side *they want* you to see."

I was pretty sure this wisdom came from CBS's Wednesday-night television lineup, either the blind detective or the clairvoyant forensic investigator.

There was no arguing with Granny, of course. My father used to try, and all he'd ever gotten for it was knockdown, drag-out grief. Their last fight had been over which side of the garage he parked on. Granny—living with my parents at the time—complained she was always banging her knee against the watering cans. Also, the fertilizer stank. Couldn't he switch sides with my mother?

Dad refused. He said he would've had to rearrange half his tools, and explained to me privately that he knew his mother: if you gave her an inch today, she was sure to take a mile tomorrow.

The conflict snowballed. She began icing her knee after car trips. They stopped talking. As the family peacemaker, I offered Granny our extra room in New Jersey. Fresh off my second divorce, I thought another adult presence would help the kids—and assumed the animosity would blow over and she'd soon be packing up her nightie and slippers and moving back in with my parents.

That was five years ago.

Now I scraped plates and loaded the dishwasher, thinking about the case. Considering my next move. Was I really going to march down to We Will Rise! after dark like I'd told Art? To make a point, prove I was tough?

There was no special link between the tutoring center and Kent Kirkland. The urgency I'd felt after glimpsing that Bright Ones wrapper didn't really apply. At this point, I was just performing basic background research, not chasing some red-hot lead.

I leaned to set a fork into the silverware caddy and missed. It landed underneath the dishwasher's propeller-ish thing, that impossible-to-reach spot where food fuzz gets soapy and gross.

I didn't go to We Will Rise! that night. Letting my downer of a meal with Art Judd fade from memory, I played an intense game of Candy Land with the kids before putting them to bed. Then I sat in the kitchen with a glass of water and thought.

You could dissect the case from a dozen different angles,

but it came down to this: Did I believe Kent Kirkland had done this awful thing?

If this were a Third Chance Enterprises mission, there would be some wild twist. Martha's husband would actually have the boys squirreled away under her nose, or Kirkland would be the tip of the iceberg to an international plot to kidnap all children possessing some genetic mutation that contained the key to immortality.

If I were in an Agatha Christie book, Miss Marple would be meticulously investigating six or seven colorful suspects, following a trail of clues toward the truth.

I didn't have six or seven suspects. I had one. And every clue I turned up seemed to take me sideways, to crumble in the face of contrary facts or opinions. Either Martha was correct and I was racing to uncover a horrible crime, or those two boys were victims of unrelated, unspectacular cruelties—the stuff of real life.

I thought for three days. When Martha called on the second, I told her I was still surveilling Kirkland even though I wasn't.

I heard nothing from Art.

Jennie, the neighborhood friend I've known since Mommy and Me art classes with Zach, was hosting bunco the third night. I tried begging out, explaining that I had a lot on my mind.

"That's why you're coming to Bunco Night!" she said.

The theme was pirates—I could wear an eye patch or one of those feathered tricorn hats.

After debating back and forth, I did go. I found a bandanna and managed to squeeze into the blouse shirt of Zach's *Pirates of the Caribbean* costume from two Halloweens ago. Meeting me at the door, Jennie shrieked and threw her arms—well, one arm and a hook —around me.

I met a few familiar faces inside, including Dawn and Meilin from Boody Burn Boot Camp. They called out, "Boody, boody, boody *bu-uuu-urn!*" by way of greeting, echoing our instructor's peppy chatter.

"Boody, boody burn," I answered sheepishly.

Jennie explained I was starting at the low table, and introduced me to my first partner, a fellow nurse at Morristown General bearing a plastic long sword.

We ate pirate-ship sandwiches (romaine leaves sticking up like sails) and drank grog (rum, lime, maybe brown sugar) out of skull-and-crossbones goblets. I started out hesitant, feeling guilty for celebrating lucky dice rolls with two boys' lives hanging in the balance, but my outlook improved as the night went on.

People asked Jennie about her neighborhood magazine idea, which she'd had in the works for months. She wanted to begin publishing a short glossy with community-interest pieces, new neighbor profiles, restaurant recommendations, et cetera.

"Getting closer, yeah!" Jennie said. "I really want to nail down the name, but nothing's speaking to me yet."

We tried helping her out. *News of Morristown? Morristown Missives?* Deb, who worked as a hairdresser in Livingston, drew hearty laughs for *Morristown Moxie.*

My first partner—with the long sword—talked about fixing a clueless doctor's charts for him at the hospital. An older woman, Jennie's son's third-grade teacher from years ago, read parts of a letter to the editor she'd written about the city council's decision to convert Devon Street into a permanent one way. All agreed the decision was ludicrous. Hadn't they ever been down to the farmer's market on a Saturday and seen all the westbound traffic?

Listening to the other ladies, accepting my third fill-up of grog, I felt myself growing into the theme.

Pirates don't care about your rules. If Art Judd told a pirate her hunch was wrong, no way was that merchant ship in the spyglass carrying slaves and ill-gotten treasure in its holds, would the pirate listen? Would she slink around belowdecks doubting herself, conceding he had a point—that, judging strictly by the outside, you couldn't truly know?

Not a chance. She'd go after that ship. And if lily-livered Art Judd didn't like it, she'd send him straight to Davy Jones's locker.

(*The bottom of the ocean, a euphemism for drowned or thrown-overboard sailors,* explained the adorable glossary on the back of each bunco scorecard.)

I left at nine thirty, early enough to tuck the kids in but late enough to see the prizes handed out. I didn't win any, but I did take home a *What Happens at Bunco Stays at Bunco* T-shirt for consolation.

"Thank you so much for coming!" Jennie said on the porch. "Everybody loved that story about Zach complaining you always put two left socks together when you fold his clothes."

I chuckled. "Teenagers. If we couldn't tell embarrassing stories about them, they wouldn't be worth it."

"That's the truth," she agreed.

We hugged, and I told Jennie she was amazing. "I can't believe you made a pirate jail."

Inside, Meilin was pretend-pouting behind a fishnet

partition. She'd gotten five minutes behind bars for talking about work.

"Oh, it's all Pinterest," Jennie said, but I knew better. She'd thought through the mix of personalities, tailored every aspect of the party to this group. It was no coincidence that Tabitha, the social justice warrior, always sat at a different table from Erin, a bigwig in the local chamber of commerce.

She asked if I was okay getting home.

"I'm walking," I said. It was only three blocks. "What're you up to tomorrow?"

Jennie wiped her brow dramatically. "Laying low. I'll drive the kiddos to school, get my toasted-white-chocolate frap. Then it's a whole lot of couch and home-improvement television."

I glanced at the carved-plank sign over the door. "Sounds perfect. You earned it."

But I wouldn't be meeting her at Starbucks. After drop-off, I was heading straight to We Will Rise!

CHAPTER THIRTEEN

E ven in the late morning, the streets around We Will Rise! were foreboding. Stop signs were streaked with spray paint and missing corners. My teeth rattled as I drove over potholes that made the Prius feel like the Mars rover. Parking, I noticed a pair of shoes draped over a power line, a thing I've never really understood but sensed wasn't welcoming.

I gripped my keys between my knuckles and walked forward.

Was it possible Jhonny had been kidnapped here? I imagined him waiting for a bus, a ten-year-old sitting with pinched knees on a steel seat, flinching every time a stranger passed.

The tutoring center itself was immaculate, a warehouse-style building with light beaming from a uniform row of windows. A sign over the entrance read in tall clean lettering: *We're here. You're here. You got this.*

I approached an opaque door with a buzzer, which I pressed.

"Student or tutor?" said a flat voice through a speaker.

"Neither," I said.

The speaker crackled. "Are you ESL?"

I puzzled a moment before remembering the acronym—English as a second language.

"No," I said. "I just had some questions to ask about a former student here. Jhonny Ramos."

More crackle, some rustling.

"Our privacy guidelines are strict," the voice said, "and we adhere to the letter."

I squeezed the strap of my purse, wishing I could see the face I was speaking with.

"I respect that," I said. "I— Look, I'm just trying to get the lay of the land. If I could come inside and talk to someone, see the facility, that's all I ask."

The speaker faded into quiet static. There might've been a sigh or annoyed breath.

Finally, the door buzzed. I hurried through.

We Will Rise! felt like a community center inside, open and bright, cushy chairs and kiosks with flyers. I knew instantly these people understood children. Vibrant colors, pictures of smiling faces, tactile displays kids could manipulate themselves like foam puzzles and a giant Connect Four game. The place had received lots of media attention, all of it richly deserved.

I followed a hopscotch rug to reception. A man behind a desk watched me without enthusiasm.

"Hi," I said with a brief wave. "My name is Molly McGill. Do you have a director of operations, somebody like that I could speak with?"

The receptionist was a wiry man with a goatee. His name tag said, "Zeke." He looked at his computer screen. I was about to try an offhand compliment of an elaborate chalkboard depiction of kids skipping rope—in case he'd drawn it—when an older man emerged from an office.

"We don't have a *director of operations*," he said. "But we have an Andre. Me."

I was stunned to have Andre Wilcox—the founder and visionary behind We Will Rise!—bustling toward me. He gave some instruction to a school-aged boy who'd followed him out of the office, clapping the boy's shoulder, then gave me his full attention.

"Mr. Wilcox," I said. "Wow. I had no idea you'd be so involved in the day-to-day."

A vigorous man with rolled-up shirtsleeves, Andre ushered me toward his office.

"The volunteers and the kids themselves run this place, I just take credit," he said. "I overheard you on the intercom. What's your angle with Jhonny?"

I explained that I was a private investigator working a theory that Jhonny was still in the area, not in Venezuela as the police believed. Andre Wilcox picked a baseball off his desk as he listened, spinning it in his fingertips.

"Know how many kids I've had go missing?" he asked. "In the six years we've been doing this?"

I shook my head.

"Thirteen," he said.

"That's awful."

"Indeed. And guess how many reporters and PIs I had come ask me about the others—ones who didn't make the nightly news?"

I grimaced, taking his point. "I'm sure it's frustrating."

He replaced the baseball on his desk. "It is what it is. We got enough to do, we just keep on truckin'."

The walls behind Andre were decorated with plaques and awards—Morristown Entrepreneur of the Year, Jersey Cares Top 40 Under 40. It was a testament to his commitment that he hadn't moved We Will Rise! to snazzier digs. He surely could've raised enough money to be anywhere.

I asked, "How many students do you help here?"

"Depends on the time of year," he said. "We're usually in the six, seven, hundreds."

"That's great. And anyone can come?"

He spread his arms. "Anyone at all. An open mind, a will to succeed—that's all we require."

I bit the corner of my lip. "You take teens?"

"We do. All the way from little squirts like Jhonny up to high schoolers."

"High schoolers with algebra issues?"

Andre Wilcox grinned. "We help kids solve more quadratic equations than a Casio calculator."

I laughed, and wondered for a moment how Zach would do here.

"Getting back to Jhonny," I said. "Is it okay if I ask a few questions? I know your receptionist mentioned privacy policies."

"As long as we stay away from personal identifying details." Andre glanced out through his office door and said in a low voice, "Zeke gets touchy sometimes. Spends all day dealing with crap."

"I know the feeling," I said.

Andre said Jhonny Ramos had been a gentle kid, quiet at first, well liked by the staff. He'd struggled with a few of their tutors but finally hit it off with one. Andre had forgotten the name, but he could track it down. Jhonny was nuts about baseball. His favorite player was José Altuve, the Astros' second baseman.

"Altuve's Venezuelan," Andre said. "He identified with his father's country. That was important to him."

This felt a bit like supporting evidence for the theory that Jhonny was in Venezuela.

"We Will Rise! is the last place he was seen," I said. "Is it possible he ran into trouble getting on the bus?"

"No," Andre said forcefully. "The bus stop's only half a block, and this neighborhood's safer than you think." I must not have looked convinced because he added, standing from his desk, "Plus, we never send our bus kids out alone at night. Either Zeke or the tutor walks them to the stop, waits with them."

I jotted this in my notebook. "As far as other students, Jhonny got along okay? No enemies?"

"Nope," Andre said. "He kept his head down. I never heard of him getting mixed up with fights, any interpersonal-type things."

"Are those issues common?"

"Not common. But you put X number of kids under one roof, it's inevitable you get some. Like that other kid who made the news—Witt. Man, he'd be rolling around the tile, wrestling somebody every damn night."

That word "Witt" hit my brain like a bell.

"Calvin Witt?" I said. "Calvin Witt came here?"

"Just for a few weeks." Andre blew sideways out of his mouth. "We give kids chances, plenty. Especially the youngsters like Calvin. But he ran right through 'em."

I felt my face contorting as I fought to contain my reaction. This was big.

"He—but his parents, I thought there was a lot of neglect. They sent him here?"

"*They* didn't," Wilcox said. "He tagged along with some kids who came down from the Ferguson place, up in Yancy Park."

"He lived there?"

"Off and on, as I understand. They aren't exactly taking attendance up there."

He described the Ferguson place as half flophouse, half foster scam. Vincent and Maeve, the couple who owned it, allowed transients and drifters to live there for next to nothing, and collected state money on as many fosters as they could cram into these second- and third-story bedrooms.

"That's awful," I said. "Why would they do that?"

Andre shrugged. "People say it's a hippie thing, peace and love. No rules."

"I guess for adults, whatever. But *foster kids*? Could they not have any of their own?"

"Nah, she had a kid years ago. It's a second marriage for her. I dunno. I stay out of other people's heads."

"That's a good practice." I tried imagining what it must've been like for Calvin, for any of those kids, fending for themselves in that oversized rattrap. "Why would any caseworker put a child there?"

"I'm with you. What I hear, they've got friends in high places with social services. Friends who look the other way."

There were voices and whistling coming from reception. Andre Wilcox glanced through his door glass, had been stealing glances for a few minutes. He probably needed to return to his duties.

I tried to think what else I should ask. I'd learned a lot—

about Jhonny's progress here, about We Will Rise!'s safety procedures, the bombshell that Calvin Witt had come here. The tutoring center served a large portion of the town's at-risk youth, but it still seemed a mighty coincidence that both missing boys had passed through here, however briefly.

"Ooh!" I remembered, gathering myself to go. "You said you could find me that tutor's name?"

Andre Wilcox started for his office door. "Absolutely. Yeah, he worked out—real thorough guy. Had a weird name."

I said, "Was it Kirkland? Kent Kirkland?"

Twisting the doorknob, Andre said, "No, that wasn't it. Here, lemme get the file off Zeke."

Deflated, I followed him out to reception where Zeke was checking in a group of kids. They were giggling and jostling each other. He asked one to confirm her street address but the girl didn't hear.

Andre sneaked behind him to the file cabinet. "Zeke, which drawer has that master list?"

Zeke broke off scowling at the kids, who'd just knocked over a stack of pamphlets, to pull out a bottom drawer. Andre slapped the smaller man's back in thanks and began flipping through manila folders.

As I waited for the name, I thought about where the case went next. The Ferguson place was near Kent Kirkland's neighborhood. I could pay them a visit, learn more about Calvin Witt's experience there—though given Andre's account, I didn't expect much help from the Fergusons. I could report back to Martha. I could report back to Becky Ramos, who would be gratified to hear how well Jhonny had been doing. The information I'd gathered here was useful but not earth-shattering, nothing that was likely to budge Art Judd off his belief that Jhonny was in Venezuela and Calvin had met a poor end at the hands of his parents.

"Whup, here we go," Andre Wilcox said, snapping a page. "Looks like Zeke stuck 'em in the wrong folder."

He was joking. The receptionist didn't smile.

Andre flattened the page on a counter between us. It was divided into five sections, each corresponding to a student. The *Jhonny Ramos* section was at the bottom.

"See there," Andre said, "he went through four tutors, each lasted a couple weeks." Start and end dates were listed in separate columns. "Then, finally, we found the right guy for him."

I followed Andre Wilcox's finger down the page to the last name, which was printed in a neat, straight script. It took me a second to place.

And then cymbals began clanging in my head.

Knut Terwilliger.

CHAPTER FOURTEEN

I blanked out for ten seconds, or three, or eighteen—I wasn't sure.

"Miss McGill," Andre Wilcox said. "Are you okay? Can I get you some water?" He glanced back to Zeke, who watched me with a one-eyed squint.

"No, no water," I said, bracing myself by the counter. "I just—I haven't eaten lunch, it hit me all of a sudden."

He closed up the folder with the tutor list and replaced it in the file cabinet. "We've got a snack machine, or I can walk you up the block to Smitty's Deli—"

"Thanks but I need to get home," I said. "My kids, they're probably halfway through the graham crackers by now. I appreciate all the great info!"

And I scampered out of We Will Rise! back to my car. I hurried into the driver's seat and locked all the doors. Only then did it occur to me I could've told Andre about Kent Kirkland, about the man behind Knut Terwilliger.

Should I have? Was it possible Kirkland still tutored at We Will Rise!? Surely not, now that he'd achieved his goal and ensnared the boys. Still, I would have to clue Andre in later to be absolutely certain no more children came into contact with him.

Right now, right this second, I had to help Jhonny and Calvin.

I hadn't seen Calvin's tutor list, but there could be no doubt Knut Terwilliger was on it. Kirkland had tutored Jhonny the night he'd gone missing. Had he taken Calvin the same way? Or nabbed Calvin from the Ferguson place somehow? It didn't matter. The detectives could sort it out later once the boys were safe.

I snatched my phone from my purse to call Art Judd. When I swiped my security pattern, the screen stayed dim. I raised it to my face.

Two percent battery.

I groaned and thumbed through my recent apps. There it was, right at the top: SparklePopper. Karen had tapped and pinched and unpinched all the way to level seventy-three. She must've been playing all morning.

I found Art's number and dialed anyway. The phone was three years old and sometimes died spontaneously below 5 percent—I had to try, though.

I got a dial tone.

Then a ring.

Then a second, third, and fourth ring.

"You've reached the voice mail for Art Judd of the Yancy Park Police Department. I'm not around, but if you'll kindly leave your information, I will check back as soon as I'm able."

Every second the message played felt like ten—my phone wasn't going to last. I started talking before the beep finished.

"Hey Art, it's me, Molly," I gushed. "I'm down at We Will Rise! and I just confirmed Kent Kirkland was Jhonny Ramos's tutor. It—er, he uses this alias to write nasty online reviews, Martha discovered it"—*shoot, why did you mention that?*—"and anyway, Calvin Witt came here too. Please call me back immediately. I'm going..."

Where *was* I going?

"...to see what I can do. You probably don't want to talk to me after the other night, but please do call. It's urgent. Obviously."

I hung up wincing at my rambling word choice. I dropped the phone onto the passenger seat, and before I'd formed my first thought about where to go, the sinking *beep-boop* tone announced its demise. I breathed a sigh of relief that I'd gotten the call in. Then I remembered, with screaming clarity, what I'd asked Art Judd to do.

Please call me back immediately.

Please do call.

But he couldn't call me back now. My line would go straight to voice mail. Maybe that was why he hadn't answered; his phone had died. Maybe every phone in the world was dead and nobody could talk to anybody and Kent Kirkland was going to figure out I was onto him before...

Stop, I told myself. *Stop and breathe.*

I fixed my hands on the steering wheel. Okay. I'd relayed the important information to Art. So what if he tried calling and got my voice mail? He would understand the gravity of the situation. He would understand that a direct connection between Kent Kirkland and the night of Jhonny's disappearance changed everything. Wasn't there a good chance he'd hop in a squad car and burn rubber out to Kirkland's the second he heard my message?

I didn't know. I hoped so.

Unsure where I was heading, I put the car in gear and drove north away from We Will Rise! Home, Martha's, Kent Kirkland's—they were all north. I hit traffic on Lockerbie, a snarl of cars behind a stalled truck, and felt almost grateful for the pause.

Now. *What am I doing?* I still owned the gun Durwood had given me at the height of the Anarchy, when you couldn't walk two city blocks without encountering a building in flames. I could retrieve it from the basement safe and go straight to the boys. Liberate them. This felt just, but also reckless and illegal.

The stalled truck was loaded onto the back of a flatbed trailer, and traffic began to flow. Before accelerating, I checked my phone instinctively for messages and found it still dead.

SparklePopper. *Ugh!*

I decided in the next block to drive to Martha's. She lived close to Kirkland. She knew the story and wouldn't require fifteen minutes of explanation like some police precinct clerk or one of my Third Chance partners, who both lived thousands of miles away regardless.

Plus, Martha had started this investigation. She'd bankrolled it from her own personal savings. She deserved to know.

I parked on the street and jogged through her lawn. I banged the door with my fist.

"Martha, we got him!" I called inside. "I found the link!"

She answered the door wearing yoga pants and a head-band. "You got me in the middle of Pilates, I'm sorry—"

"Kent Kirkland was Jhonny's tutor." I gripped her forearm, which was damp with sweat. "That online alias you found was the key."

As I entered and gave my news, Martha listened with a complex expression. Her hazel eyes rounded in surprise, then what seemed like wonder. Her mouth set determinedly, but did one corner twitch up in affirmation?

"He tutored them," she repeated, staring vacantly into her kitchen's repeating-utensil wallpaper. "It doesn't get more diabolical than that."

I nodded agreement. The thought occurred to me, though, that Kirkland had helped Jhonny at We Will Rise! What was that Andre Wilcox had said, that Jhonny had "finally hit it off" with him? What about those other students he'd helped—and not kidnapped?

"I already called Art Judd," I said.

Martha's brow crimped.

I clarified, "That detective? I talked to him right after I took the case?"

"Right, him," she said, then, slyly: "Last time we talked, you two had a little something going."

I couldn't remember quite what I'd said, but apparently it hadn't been discreet.

"Yeah, things have cooled since then," I said. "But he's more or less in the loop, and I left him a message about Kirkland. Or, you know, about Knut Terwilliger."

"What did he say?"

"I don't know," I said. "My phone's dead so he can't call me back."

This seemed to flummox Martha. She looked to her own cell. "Don't you think he would? I mean, if you had feelings for a person who left a message saying—"

"I don't know that he actually does have feelings for—"

"—saying all those things, saying she'd done this brilliant investigation and knew the whereabouts of two kidnapped boys. Wouldn't you call?"

I rolled my tongue around my cheek, considering.

"I would," I said. "And you would. But would Art Judd?"

We both studied her hardwood floor.

I said, "It doesn't matter, we can't sit around wondering. We have to get help. Now."

I looked up at Martha, but the words from my own mouth had changed her. Suddenly, she wasn't Martha. She was my mother.

We have to get help. Now.

My father had used this exact phrase twenty-five years ago, on the backside of a mountain my family used to ski together in Vermont. We went there because it was cheap and Dad liked that highway 5 was divided most of the way there—but that day, his safety calculations hadn't worked out. An out-of-control snowboarder had slammed into me two turns off the lift, and I was lying in a twisted heap in the snow.

"I'll stay with her," my mother said.

"No, you can get to the medical tent faster," said Dad, the weaker skier of the two.

He hid his mouth, but I still heard him add, "*She needs an airlift.*"

My mother squared her face to mine and said not to worry, it'd be fine. I was crying and shivering. I tried nodding but immediately felt a searing pain near my shoulder, like the worst tooth pain transplanted into my torso. I was afraid I would end up paralyzed or lose fingers to frostbite. I had the wild thought Mom would chase down the snowboarder and he'd end up having a weapon in his backpack and hurt her.

"What if—what if I can't move?" I asked. "What if we're stuck here?"

Her eyes traveled down my body and back up, and somehow, without sparing a second, she managed to slow down the moment.

"We're going to manage," she said. "But your brothers are probably going to brag about making it to the bottom first."

My smile just did touch the pain—which turned out to be a broken collarbone—before vanishing from my blubbering lips.

She did make it to the medical tent quickly, and in a matter of minutes, I was strapped securely to a rescue toboggan and traversed down the mountain to care. I didn't need an airlift. The medic stabilized me as my parents pressed hot packs into my hands and my brother Greg chewed his ski gloves. I rode in an ambulance to the nearest hospital, where I got a bunch of X-rays and a sling for three weeks.

Still, I wasn't the same after the ordeal. We kept skiing but I never dug my edges into the snow with quite the same conviction, never breezed into my turns with that weightless wonder you're supposed to feel on the slopes. I continued to enjoy the sport, but I wouldn't become a ski bum like Greg or put my toddlers into perfect-turn lessons like Nate. Whereas they stayed north for college, I headed south to New Jersey, where I met Zach's father at Rutgers and eventually settled.

The snowboarder who sideswiped me didn't doom me

to my fate—doom me to Morristown. I love Morristown. But he did change things. These moments matter, these traumas and how we deal with them.

Martha was gripping the arm of her couch, resolute.

"We can use my phone," she said. "Call nine-one-one, don't you think?"

I gazed down the block toward Kirkland's house. An emergency dispatcher would probably send a squad car here, to Martha's house, then we would have to sell our story about Kirkland to the officer. It might be quicker to just wait for Art to check his messages.

But what if Art already had checked his messages? What if he wasn't impressed?

"Nine-one-one, yes," I said. "We just can't count on—"

The doorbell interrupted—sudden, harsh—before I could explain what we couldn't count on.

CHAPTER FIFTEEN

All five senses are intricately linked to cognition. A bite of vanilla sheet cake in an empty bakery tastes different from the same bite taken before a hundred cheering friends and family in your wedding dress. The sight of a geriatric man with a shaggy white beard evokes one reaction when he's wearing rags and another when the same face appears under a red hat with a white pom-pom.

When I heard Martha Dodson's doorbell now—come straight from We Will Rise!, waiting urgently to hear from a detective—it hit the auditory cortex of my brain like hungry wolves snarling. My stomach clenched and I shrank from the noise.

"The kitchen window!" Martha said, reacting similarly. "We can see who it is from there."

I followed her on light feet, not talking, not breathing. I knew who the visitor was. I knew it in my heart and stomach and thrumming wrists.

The window was over the sink. Martha and I came

around the island, steadying ourselves by the sink's stainless-steel fixtures, and peered out.

Kent Kirkland stood on Martha's porch, one black oxford tapping impatiently.

Martha and I dropped to the tile.

"How did he know?" she asked. "Is my house *bugged*?"

"I don't know," I said. "Maybe he..."

Could he have some source inside the police department, somebody who'd overheard my message to Art? Granny's "dirty cop"? My grandmother tossed off all sorts of wild innuendo and conspiracy theories—occasionally one found the mark.

Maybe Martha had confronted Kent Kirkland earlier and not told me. Clients did this all the time, describing their case in painstaking, comprehensive detail—all except the part where they'd been caught trying to steal back a Weedwacker from the neighbor's garage.

"He can't know," I said. "He can't. We barely know what we know ourselves."

"Then how is he here?" Martha's headband had twisted inside out over one ear.

I risked a peek outside, then ducked back down. "The Prius. He must've recognized my car and connected it to my visit somehow."

"What—but so he knows you're inside?"

"No, he *thinks* I'm inside." I moved closer to Martha and squared my face to hers. She blinked. "My car's halfway between your house and the neighbor's. You can play dumb, deny I'm here."

She blinked again. "I'm...answering the door?"

I gripped her shoulder. "It has to be you."

In another heartbeat, the doorbell buzzed again.

Scrambling, we decided I would hide in the mudroom closet, which couldn't be seen from the front door. We held each other's gaze for a last moment before splitting off.

Be careful, I mouthed.

A shaky breath filled her chest. *I will.*

The closet wasn't roomy. I squatted in the left-hand side, which had more clearance than the right—Martha had stored old kids' coats on this end of the rod. I pressed myself in among shoeboxes and clear tubs of papers and electrical cords, and pulled the door shut.

Martha's footsteps were already faint when I remembered nine-one-one. I felt around for my phone, but it was in the car, out of juice.

Dang. I should've taken Martha's or borrowed her charger.

I wondered where her closest home phone was. The kitchen?

Could there be a loose handset floating around the hall?

I heard the front door open, then Martha: "May I help you?"

Kent Kirkland's voice was muted through the closet door but just as insistent as I remembered.

"Where is she?" he said. "The woman with the Prius?"

"Excuse me, who?"

"The woman, the car!" I imagined him pointing a quavering finger toward the street. "I recognize that car. It's been to my home."

"That silver one?" Martha said. "Hm, I don't know it. Must be a visitor of my neighbor's."

She was doing a great job staying composed, judging by her voice, at least.

But Kirkland wasn't buying. "The car is clearly parked

adjacent to your property. It's three feet inside the cobble-stone pavers."

"Oh, those pavers belong to the Burtlesons. That isn't the property line."

I heard nothing for a few seconds. The closet had a close medicinal odor, maybe bug spray from the outgrown jackets. Something like a shoelace brushed my shin.

Kirkland, apparently after a closer look at the neighbors' house, said, "The lights are off inside. There's a rolled-up advertisement on the doorknob."

Martha tittered, short and brittle.

Be strong, I thought. *Stick to your story.*

Kirkland continued, "I don't know how you're mixed up with that woman, but I'll tell you something about her. She came to my house—my home—and harassed me. She said she was from the Northern New Jersey Horticultural Society."

"That's a lovely organization," Martha said.

"It's a scam. She was pushing these exotic seeds, these *organic* seeds that cost a fortune."

"Organic seeds can be expensive."

"They're a crock."

"I beg to differ there," Martha said, and I began feeling queasy about the exchange. She should've been pushing for him to leave—a stranger asking after a person supposedly not at her house. It wasn't in Martha's nature to be rude, but rude would've been most believable here.

She went on, "I've grown organic and conventional seeds side by side, and organic outperformed."

From within the closet, I just did hear Kirkland's derisive snort.

"I suppose you did a rain dance as well."

"No, I was skeptical too," Martha said. "But the premium is justified. I'd buy with confidence from the horticultural society."

Her voice was full of defense for me, and I smiled despite our shared danger. That shoelace tickled my shin again.

Kirkland said, "I have my doubts that this woman has any connection at all to gardening. Twenty-four dollars a packet for seeds."

"That's not unreasonable. Even for flowering seeds—organic methods are expensive, whether you eat the plant's bounty or not."

Martha broke off abruptly, as though something were happening I couldn't see. I crouched closer to the door. A tiny mew startled me. I looked down into the bright eyes of a cat, whose tail—not a shoelace—switched near my shin.

"Shh," I whispered.

Kent Kirkland's next words were low, taut: "I never said she was selling flowering seeds."

Panic bloomed through me, pushing my heart to a gallop. I staggered from my squat. The cat hissed.

Martha stuttered, "I—I was only speaking hypo-thetically—"

"She's inside," Kirkland interrupted. "You and I both know it."

Martha shrieked, but the cry was quickly silenced. In its place came clomping footsteps and the sounds of struggle.

CHAPTER SIXTEEN

My first instinct was to bolt from the closet and help Martha. To rush Kirkland, tackle him, rake my nails through his eyes so Martha could at least escape. Maybe she'd get to a phone and dial nine-one-one.

I felt around for a weapon—ice pick, broom, anything—but came up empty. There was also the problem of distance. The closet could've been fifteen feet from the front door. If Kirkland heard me coming, or saw me, I was in trouble.

I decided to wait until they came closer. I listened to the scrabbling, grunting, heaving fight, both my hands tight around the closet door's inner knob.

"Where is she?" Kirkland roared. "Tell me!"

They were about halfway to me, I judged by sound. The cat had picked up on my stress, scurrying back and forth at my feet.

"I don't know, *I don't know*," Martha said.

"Yes, you do!"

I flexed forward on one knee, preparing to go, but then the struggling stopped. I heard the squeak of a door—interior, to a study or dining room. Then a groan and sliding shoes.

Is he dragging her?

Kirkland's next words were muffled and came from my left.

"What the... How're you, er, that's my picture!"

Now I knew which room they were in: the one where Martha had erected her TV-crime-drama-style bulletin board.

Martha answered with new strength, seeming to decide the jig was up. "You do have those boys, we were right. Molly found the proof. You took them from the tutoring center."

"That's absurd."

"You tutored Jhonny Ramos. You pretended to help him."

"I *did* help him."

"No," Martha insisted, "you became an important figure in his life, and then you exploited that position to—"

"I *saved* those boys!" Kirkland said, apparently undone by her damning words. "Look at them—look at those pictures." He must've been indicating Martha's newspaper photos. "Jhonny's wearing rags. Calvin looks like a whale."

"Children have all different body types, that doesn't—"

"Nobody gets that size without a steady supply of *sugar* and *processed junk*." Kirkland's outrage penetrated the closet wall, reaching deep into my gut. "I fed him properly. I got him a scooter for exercise. I've probably increased his life expectancy by a decade."

Martha faltered answering him. She must've been feeling what I was—shock and horror at Kirkland's revelations. I thought about those tomato plants and bell pepper seedlings in his grow room. About that UPS box Martha had rightly guessed contained a scooter.

"Jh-Jhonny's mother," she said. "Can you even imagine her pain?"

"She had ten years to be a mother," Kirkland said. "Ten years. She forfeited the right."

"No," Martha said. "No, you took her right. Those boys, you just... They...they're prisoners!"

"We're all prisoners," Kirkland said, gravel in his tone.

Danger pulsed through the house, in the floorboards and air. My eardrums sizzled. Each of Kirkland's justifications slipped neatly into place with what I'd learned about him—the worship of order, his severe judgments, his positive impact at We Will Rise! He believed he was in the right. Society had failed these boys, and he'd fixed it.

I remembered what he'd said about those messy cookbooks in his kitchen. *Books deserve to be free.* But apparently not children.

When a mind can twist the world this grotesquely, there's no place it can't go.

The doorbell rang.

Five minutes ago, the noise had been dreadful; now it sounded like grace. Martha and Kirkland's argument stopped. I held my breath, praying whoever it was didn't leave.

Should I sprint to the door and answer?

The doorbell rang again.

Now Kirkland resumed, strangled, "Ignore it. They'll leave."

I couldn't hear Martha's answer. In the dark below, the cat whimpered.

Shh, I mouthed.

Three smacks sounded on the door, then: "Mrs. Dodson, this is Art Judd of the Yancy Park Police Department. I need to speak with you, please."

A sharp breath through the wall could've been Martha or Kirkland—hope, or anger.

"Don't...make...a sound," Kirkland said.

For thirty seconds, the house was silent. I felt overjoyed that Art had come, that he'd taken my message seriously, but how could we get him to break in and help? He must've tried calling me back, then driven out here and found my car in front of Martha's house. Like Kent Kirkland had.

Was Kirkland's car in front of the house too? Or had he walked? I couldn't remember—we'd only peeked quickly from the window.

In the small, dark closet, scenarios spiraled around my head. Was Art drawing his gun? Did Kirkland have one himself? I wondered again how Kirkland had ended up here, whether he'd tracked my car or gotten help from Granny's dirty cop.

Martha's cat interrupted with a loud meow.

I shushed her again. She meowed louder. Twice.

I gritted my teeth and screamed inside my head for it to *be quiet!* Cats are amazing companions—there's nothing better for a rainy Sunday afternoon than one curled in your lap and a Danielle Steel novel—but they can be downright maddening. When Karen was a baby, Simba had the habit of jumping into her crib at the precise moment I'd coaxed my light-sleeping daughter's eyes to flutter closed.

Through the wall, Kirkland hissed, "What's that sound?"

"My cat," Martha said.

"She'll give us away!"

"Do you want me to, um, go find her? Sometimes she catches mice and wants to show them to me."

Kirkland snapped that, no, he didn't want her doing one single thing. Meanwhile, the cat was watching me with its piercing eyes, surely about to talk again. I reached out to scratch under its chin—that's usually what Simba wants—and accidentally nudged a stack of boxes.

They crashed.

There was movement through the wall but no words. Was Kirkland coming toward the noise? Would he risk popping out to the hall in pursuit and exposing himself to Art? I didn't think so.

But Art hadn't knocked for a while.

Had he gone?

All I could see to do was stay crouched in place, as quiet as possible, and wait. And pray.

The contents of one shoebox had spilled by the door, such that I could see them by the hallway light fuzzing underneath.

They were mementos. A four-by-six of Martha at a high school dance, beaming, her brown hair feathered. A toddler in pigtails held aloft by an elderly man (her grandfather?) wearing a checkered suit. I teared up despite the predicament. I'm an absolute sucker for pictures of people changing through the years.

At the back was a news article clipped to a stack of handwritten letters. I squinted at the headline. "Neighborhood Matron's Drunk Driving Was Known, Tolerated." The article, from a suburban Philadelphia paper, described an eighty-six-year-old widow's frequent jaunts through her subdivision after wine-soaked afternoons, times she'd taken out mailboxes or sideswiped trees, how it was a running joke among the families on her block—until she killed a teenage boy backing out of her drive, plugging the gas in reverse without a backward glance.

The boy's name, Josh Brewer, meant nothing to me until I read the final line of the article.

"The young Mr. Brewer is survived by his parents, Jim and Anastasia, and sister Martha."

The attached letters were addressed to either "Jim and Ana" or "The Brewer Family." I thought about Martha's floor loom, made by her brother, as I read the neighbors' condolences.

He was a lovely boy. I'll miss seeing him look up and wave when he was mowing the grass.

We are so very sorry, and wish to personally apologize for Josh's death. Fay's drinking could've been stopped. It should've been.

The letters were spread at the bottom of the door—I'd nudged the stack apart with one knuckle. The last was written on a torn spiral page with frayed edges. I read it, shaking on my knees.

I can't believe my wife and I used to joke about it. 'The Car Bowling Hour,' we used to call it, around four o'clock. I would give anything to go back in time and do the responsible thing.

CHAPTER SEVENTEEN

My heart felt swollen. I imagined Martha—middle-school Martha—attending her brother's funeral, covering her face and shrinking from the coffin. I imagined her tiptoeing out into the world at college. How had it affected her? Did she play it safer socially, sticking close to her hallmates, dating the boys who seemed least likely to disappear?

I imagined her looking out the window at Kent Kirkland hacking his begonias, feeling in her bones that something was wrong—and nobody else knew.

"Mrs. Dodson, if you're there," Art called loudly through the front door. "I need to get inside. I'm gonna call for backup, then I'm breaking down the door."

He knows we're at risk. He saw my car.

Through the wall, panting and bustling.

"Go, go answer!" Kirkland commanded Martha. "Tell him everything is fine..."

He gave more instructions, but I couldn't hear, and soon they were leaving the room for the hall. Some table or stand fell. It seemed Kirkland had forgotten my own crash in his hurry. He must've realized that if Art called for backup, it was all over.

One set of footsteps continued to the front door, softer than Kirkland's *clip-clopping* oxfords. What would Martha do? Would she stick to her captor's script? Would she try to communicate our distress to Art without Kirkland noticing?

I needed to be ready. If it came to a standoff, if I moved fast, I might be able to catch Kirkland from behind.

Again, I looked around for a weapon. I'd made a mess of the closet—Martha's cat was hunting around gingerly, sniffing—and more objects were in view. An umbrella, but just a mini. A pair of outlet splitters sprawled like dice. This was the sort of space that might've taken a canister fire extinguisher, which would've done nicely, but I didn't see one.

Martha's voice sounded unnaturally bright. "Good afternoon, Detective. How can I help you?"

There was a pause. I wondered how their eyes looked, if some silent conversation was happening there.

Art said, "Took you a while to get the door. Everything okay inside?"

"Oh yes, yes." Martha tittered. "I was just back in the, uh, laundry room. Laundry. Hanging my delicates."

I pressed my ear to the closet door, listening to the exchange but also for Kirkland. Was he crouched behind Martha, preparing to strike? Looking for another exit to sneak out, some side door?

Looking for me?

Art asked, "Where's Molly? She called me, and I see her car's out front."

"She called, did she? What did she say?"

"She said you'd tied Kirkland to the missing boys. Something about him using an alias."

Martha took her time answering. I could sense her calculating, trying to thread the needle between the man in front of her and the man behind.

Art prompted, "So is she inside, Molly?"

"No!" Martha said. "No, she—she went to Kent Kirkland's house, for the boys."

"She did? Crap. I— Excuse me," Art said. "I need to get over there. That guy, if he's held two boys hostage all this time? I gotta go."

Shoes pounded over brick, and I cheered in my head, *Yes, go! Go break out Jhonny and Calvin!*

But Martha called, "She said you might come, she had a message."

The shoes stopped.

"A message for me?" Art said.

"Yes," Martha said. "She said to tell you she didn't want your help. You didn't believe in her before, when she told you about the granola bars. So why believe now? You broke her trust."

It was lucky I already had my ear against the door because now my forehead fell into it with hardly a noise.

What are you doing, Martha? Let him go! Or sprint away out of the house with him, anything. *Don't start lecturing him about trust.*

"Ah, sheesh," Art said. "It's true, though. I was wrong. I didn't listen. I figured I knew better."

I was frozen, nerves jumping across every inch of my body as Art—seeming to forget the situation entirely—kept talking. He admitted he'd fallen back on old habits. Cynicism. Low expectations. All the stuff that had dragged down his marriage. He just had to play the crank.

Martha put in, "I do think she has feelings for you. Even though she's upset."

"Yeah?"

"She mentioned your mustache, how it felt different but...nice."

This was absolutely insane, talking about feelings and mustaches with two boys' lives on the line.

Is Martha doing it on purpose? Buying time? Giving some nonverbal signal?

Art chuckled. "I'm different alright."

"Different is good," Martha said. "I think Molly would be open to a fresh start."

"Well, I hope you're right," he said. "Molly's a heckuva woman. When you talk to her, everything's a little sunnier. You know? She inspires it."

His rising tone sent my insides into free fall, my heart turning a slow, dreamy somersault. I imagined Art's eyes softening, and color coming into his broad cheeks.

"Yes," Martha said. "I know."

Art seemed to return to his senses then. "I'm off, I need to get over to Kirkland's place. 'Preciate your time."

"But wait!" Martha exclaimed. "Don't go, I—I lied."

"Lied?"

"Yes, I...Molly didn't go. You were actually right. She's here inside."

Again, I was at a loss. *What on earth was Martha doing?* Was she in the middle of a nervous breakdown?

"Ma'am," Art said, "I don't know if you're confused, or trying to pull some trick. Molly McGill is caught in the middle of a very dangerous situation, and if I don't reach her soon—"

The rest of his sentence was swallowed by the crack of a pump-action rifle and Kent Kirkland's voice.

"Inside, *now!*" he shouted. "Both of you on the floor."

CHAPTER EIGHTEEN

He forced them to the kitchen, presumably at gunpoint. Then he tied them up using twine Martha fetched from a cabinet. The sound each length of twine made being cut—ragged, probably with a serrated knife—raised goose bumps on my neck.

"Where's the other one?" Kirkland roared. "Where's the snoop, Molly?"

"She—she must've slipped out," Martha tried. "She knows Calvin and Jhonny are—"

"She knows nothing," Kirkland said. "She's here. You hid her when I came to the door. *Where?*"

Martha murmured indecipherably before Art came to her defense.

"Listen, we can get you outta this," the detective said. "Let's be calm. Right? Let's all breathe."

Martha shrieked. I imagined Kirkland brandishing the gun, which had to be Willard's deer rifle.

Kirkland enunciated precisely, "Where is she?"

"Mr. Kirkland, take your time here. Be reasonable."

"We're well past reason," Kirkland said, a raw streak in his voice. "You people poked around in business you shouldn't have."

"Mr. Kirkland, all these women cared about was the welfare of those two boys."

"Nonsense! I care about their welfare. I made the hard decisions, I took the risks to save them. *These women*"—he gave Art's phrase a nasal quality—"were in it for themselves. For the glory."

His misogyny made me snarl reflexively. I'd experienced it firsthand at his house. *Your husband allows it?* Hearing it come in a time of stress, this easy disdain for two women he knew nothing about, I was sure he'd suffered some hurt—real or invented—from a female in the past. His mother, a girlfriend. Somebody had damaged him.

This was no time for extended psychoanalysis, though. Kirkland had hostages and a loaded gun. His state was frazzled, gravely stressed. I might be able to leave the closet and sneak up the hall without being noticed. I might catch him with his back turned. With the right first strike, I might overpower him without the gun discharging.

It was an awful lot of "might."

"Meow! Meee-OW!"

My head shot to the noise. Martha's cat, done inspecting the mess, was peering up at me expectantly. I hurried to scratch its chin, but the cat kept vocalizing.

"Mrrow, *mrro-ooow!*" Its eyes closed pleasurably, and I felt purring through its neck. "Meow!"

"Stop!" I whispered. "I'm petting you, okay?"

But the cat only sped up its cries, sounding like some cell phone alarm. I thought about clamping my hand over its furry little mouth, but knew all I'd get was scratched to shreds and hissing just as loud as the meows.

Down the hall, Kirkland said, "That cat again!" He growled audibly. "Can't you *shut it up*?"

"Like I said, it could be a mouse," Martha said. "Or she could be out of kibble. I can fill her upstairs bowl if you untie me."

"No, *no*," Kirkland snapped. "Nobody goes upstairs. Nobody gets untied." A long pause. "I'll bet that cat is with the snoop."

Martha said, no, she doubted that, probably just—

"It's the snoop," Kirkland interrupted. "They're together."

As he started hotly down the hall, I tried again to quiet the cat. I knelt to its level. I rolled a stray tennis ball through its path.

Nothing worked.

"Meow-OW-*oww!* Mrrow..."

Kirkland's oxfords clomped closer, louder. Angrier. There was no throwing him off the scent now.

I stood up and, my chest pressing into hung coats, looked around the high shelf, the only place I hadn't checked yet for a weapon. A stack of folded gift bags in one corner. A retired dustbuster. I took the dustbuster by the handle, then, considering its snubbed mouth, put it back.

Kirkland was almost to the closet.

The shelf was mostly occupied by a bin of cleaning supplies. Scrubber brush...glass cleaner...pack of squishy Magic Erasers...lemon-scented Pledge...

The door handle jostled from outside. I gripped its inside knob.

"Open this, come out!" Kirkland demanded.

I kept my grip on the handle, twisting back to the cleaning supplies. I had to choose now. There were chemicals aplenty here, but could any of them hurt Kirkland? Stun him, at least?

Bleach.

That fuddy-duddy standby—it was my best shot. Hurriedly, I snagged the squat jug by its neck. It felt reassuringly heavy and full. Retreating to my corner again, I let go of the doorknob and twisted the cap off the bleach.

My nose filled with that sharp, aggressively fresh smell. My pulse throbbed in my wrists and temples.

On the other side of the door, Kirkland must've been gathering for a great heave. I waited. I poised my bottle of bleach.

The door flew open suddenly—there was no resistance, my hand gone.

"Argh!" Kirkland groaned, taking the impact on the nose.

The cat looked at him, said a last meow, and scampered off between his legs.

In his split second of confusion, I spilled the bleach forward toward his face. A lot splashed off his glasses, but some got behind to his eyes. He screamed, swore, rammed one palm into his eye socket. The other hand held Willard's rifle. I took a swipe for it, but when Kirkland's grip didn't yield, I gave it up and sprinted away—leaving him writhing outside the closet.

I found Art and Martha tied up in the kitchen.

"Molly!" they both cried.

I got Martha's wrists and ankles free first, breaking two nails on the knots.

Art said, "You guys run, go. Call nine-one-one."

His cheek was cut, and his body was curled like a tortured comma on the ground. I looked into his fevered eyes and couldn't help hearing his voice from a minute ago saying everything was a little sunnier with me around.

Before I could choose between running with Martha or freeing him, a blast rent the air.

Kent Kirkland staggered in from the hall. "Look, look what you made me do!"

Smoke drifted from the gun's muzzle. The wall above me had a gash in its drywall. Martha's repeating-utensil wallpaper was shredded, singed knife handles and fork tines curling black at the edges.

"Look at this mess, this...this situation!" Kirkland's left eye was pink. His right was fully red.

He was approaching his breaking point, I saw. He kicked a toppled chair away viciously and straightened a crooked runner rug underfoot. He couldn't handle this. He wasn't built for it. Order, rigor, schedule—he needed these to cope. How would he respond to disintegration?

He still had the power. A gun, one of us tied up. Would he balk at taking the next step, at making his world even messier? Would he pull up and return to sanity?

Or would he follow the chaos down?

Art said from the ground, "You did this yourself, all of it. You're a monster."

Kirkland leveled the gun barrel at the detective. "I risked everything, *everything* for them! You have no idea."

"You're sick," Art said. "You're sick and you're going straight to hell."

"Shut your mouth! People like you don't underst—"

"Be a man. Let those boys go."

They argued back and forth, Art sticking with his

caveman approach. I wanted to wring his neck. Just a second ago, he'd been deescalating. *Be calm. Be reasonable.* What had gotten into him? Was he playing macho because I was here? Had he spotted some change in Kirkland that he thought called for a new approach?

"You're an officer of the law," Kirkland said, his square jaw shaking, "but you have no idea what safety is. None. The world will be better without you."

He advanced on the detective, spittle on his lip, squinting down the barrel.

Art's face screwed up stubbornly, and I knew he was about to make things worse.

"Kent, wait!" I said, lunging between them. "I know you think—er, you believe those boys' lives are better because of your..." I struggled for a word. "Your actions. Isn't that right?"

His finger was on the trigger. "They are. Their parents were complete and utter trash."

"They had a rough go of it, no question," I said. "But everyone goes forth under a different set of circumstances."

"Abject neglect cannot be justified. Nothing in those households explains why those children didn't receive supervision and nutrition rising to basic humanitarian levels."

His eye narrowed at the rifle sight. He fixed the runner rug again with his foot.

I circled slowly toward Art. "Fair enough—and you've provided those things." I gulped against my true distaste. "And now—now, when they return to their families, Jhonny and Calvin will be poised for success."

"No," he said. "Those parents...no child could succeed."

"I've spent a bit of time with Jhonny's mother, and honestly I think she—"

"A parent who doesn't care about a nine-year-old doesn't magically start caring about a ten-year-old!"

A muscle in his neck began twitching. He shrugged his shoulder on that side as though to control it, but the spasm continued.

I said, "People change. I'm going to venture out on a limb here and guess that your parents—"

"My parents were exactly the same," Kirkland snapped. "Yes! Yes they were, and I only wish somebody would've had the guts to do the same. To rescue *me*!"

Martha—across the runner rug from me—gasped. Art's thumbs were working on his ties behind his back.

"If you had been taken from them. From your parents," I said, measuring my words, "I'm sure they would've been sad."

"Doubtful."

"Kent, what appears true in childhood—"

"Go ask them!" He lowered the gun to glower at me, and I thought for a moment Art might take the chance to attack—but quickly, Kirkland swung the barrel threateningly about the kitchen. "Go on, mother's just up the road. Ask her!"

We followed his eyes to the window, through Martha's curtains, and up the hill.

The Ferguson place.

"That's right," he continued into our stunned silence. "I grew up with stacks of junk mail outside my bedroom door. And strangers soiling our toilet seat. And puke, and fleas, and every page of homework I ever brought home dumped together with greasy fast-food wrappers. My father left. *Escaped.* I didn't have that luxury."

Kirkland railed for a minute straight on the place's horrors, echoing and expanding what I'd heard from Andre Wilcox. His stiff voice cracked and fell off to a trickle, then came booming back. His bleach-irritated eyes pinched and popped. The gun barrel continued to whip around.

I had the awful thought that if he killed us, he would take his own life next.

"That sounds horribly unfair," I said. "Nobody should endure such things."

My mind was in overdrive. I needed to place Jhonny's and Calvin's stories in the context of his. Of his pain. It was the only way to help him see his own delusions.

He sniffed hard. "I walked the halls of my grade school with lice—*with nits eating my scalp.* Nobody cared. Nobody stopped it."

I remembered Art saying at Pi's Sushi that he'd been truant in elementary school.

"People can be hesitant to overstep," I said, then when his expression darkened: "Which is no excuse, of course. You're right, we have to help at-risk kids. But we need to *listen* to them and figure out—"

"Stop talking!" Kirkland said. "I don't need you unpacking a bunch of psychobabble." He jerked the gun. "Down! Down on the floor with him."

He gave the same instruction to Martha, and we complied, lowering ourselves to the hardwood. Kirkland grabbed the spool of twine he must've used before off the island. It only had a foot or two remaining. He chucked it into the trash bin, briefly rummaged for more in the drawers, then gave up with a growl.

To himself, he muttered, "Neat...neat...what would be neatest?"

His eyes traveled the room, seeking, red, raw, feral. They settled on Martha. The barrel of the rifle followed.

"It's your house." He shifted his sights to Art and me. "And the two of you are intruding."

Finally, his chest filled with a peaceful breath, and he said once more:

"Neat."

CHAPTER NINETEEN

As Martha began shivering in place and Art struggled with his ties, I kept brainstorming. *Okay.* Kirkland was planning to shoot us all and try passing it off as a botched home invasion. The scheme wouldn't work—he was no seasoned criminal who knew how to anticipate an investigation and fake evidence trails. He'd be caught. He'd spend the rest of his life in jail.

But that wouldn't do us three any good.

I would've given anything to have Sue-Ann nosing around. Durwood's geriatric bluetick coonhound had a knack for these situations. Whether it was surprising the English mercenary, Blake Leathersby, in the depths of a subterranean fortress in the Anarchy's last days, or sniffing out the ricin-filled balloon that might've killed every soul aboard a nuclear submarine in Vladivostok, Sue always managed to wriggle out of danger.

Where was Ziggy, Martha's dog? Probably in the back-yard. The only animal I'd seen in the house was her cat, who hadn't struck me as especially courageous.

What options did I have? Who would Kirkland shoot first? Art was his biggest threat superficially, but Art was bound. Martha and I weren't. If two of us attacked simultaneously, we might stand a chance. But how would we coordinate?

My elbow was resting on a corner of the runner rug— the far corner, away from Kirkland. On a hunch, I nudged it askew.

He noticed a moment later and, holding the gun aside, fixed the rug.

"Back up," he told Martha. "If this is a break-in, you should be there." He waved her toward the stand mixer. "No, *there*, to the left. Better."

As he was distracted positioning her, talking through the scenario, I nudged the rug again. Kirkland noticed as soon as he turned.

"*Damn.*" He straightened it again, stamping the spot.

Martha caught my eye.

Kirkland raised the rifle and aimed.

I needed to stall him.

"Does Calvin know you grew up there?" I asked, glancing out the window to the Ferguson place.

"Doesn't matter."

"You realize he was there, don't you?"

Kirkland ignored the question.

I said, "Is that where you took him from?"

My questions were getting under his skin. "It doesn't matter. None of this matters."

"Or from the tutoring center?"

"Shut up!" Kirkland said. "I know what you're doing, I understand your tactics. You're only wasting time."

Martha took advantage of his outburst to tease the runner rug another inch with her toe.

When Kirkland finished shouting, he saw.

"This rug!" He swore and dropped to his knees, positioning the corner again with both hands squared in right angles. "You need a pad—why don't you have a pad underneath?"

"I—I had one but it kept poking out," Martha said. "The edges got stuck in the vacuum cleaner."

"Then use tape," Kirkland snarled. "A dot of two-sided tape at each corner."

"But tape gums up the wood."

"That's what rubbing alcohol is for!"

Through the Great Rug Stabilization Debate, I scrambled for another move, some way to turn the tables. Art was staring at me intently. His cut had bled into his mustache, turning it darker.

What's he trying to communicate?

Does he have a gun? Did Kirkland take one off him, set it on the counter somewhere?

"Enough of this!" Kirkland said, steadying the rifle's barrel. "It's time. People could be on their way."

Art said slowly, "Nobody's coming. I never radioed for backup."

"I don't believe you."

"It's true. I was about to walk back to the car when Martha answered—"

"No!" Kirkland yelled. "Anyway, the boys—they must be starved. I need to prepare dinner for the boys."

His Adam's apple bobbed furiously. He was at a critical juncture. Here was a man who'd most likely never inflicted bodily hurt on another person. Mental hurt, yes. Psychological abuse and coercion, certainly. But firing a weapon and turning Martha Dodson's kitchen into a ghoulish scene of shattered bone and flesh? Could he carry out such a profound break?

I tried, "You're in control of your fate. Of our fates. Whatever your parents did or didn't do, whatever choices got us here—none of it matters. You control this moment.

"*You.*"

If my message registered, it was only for a moment. His eyes, behind the glasses' thick frames, rose to an icy, terrible peak.

Then, seeming almost entranced, he swung the gun toward Art.

Dread shot through me, but I was ready. I wedged my toe under the runner rug and kicked, making a ripple that spanned the length of the rug. The corner nearest Kirkland flopped like a dog's ear, showing an ugly latex backing.

"Stupid, *stupid* rug!" he cried.

I hoped he would set down the gun but he didn't, keeping Art in his sights, stomping sideways to the rug's center. He squatted and reached out to smooth the upended corner.

I waited for his fingers to touch the latex, the moment when his torso's weight was farthest out over his knees. Then I yanked with both hands.

Kirkland's build was slight, but standing over six feet, he could've weighed two hundred pounds. The rug stayed put at first. I quickly gathered another inch of fabric in my fists and yanked again. My shoulders strained for a sickening instant of doubt, and then, gloriously, the rug came toward me.

I toppled back. The rifle discharged as Kent Kirkland's

feet flew out from underneath. He landed on his neck, dropping the gun, his face twisted in pain and rage.

Art scrabbled no-handed to all fours—resembling Sue-Ann more than a little—and plowed his shoulder into Kirkland.

The rifle lay on the ground. Martha and I both lunged for it, our hands finding the stock at the same time.

"I got it," I said.

She smiled and let go. Art and Kent Kirkland were grappling on the ground, their heaving bodies bucking and stretching the rug below.

"Get off him, *now*!" I told Kirkland.

He was panting heavily and straddling Art, who couldn't use his hands, still bound.

"This— You— You're disrupting the dinner schedule," he said.

"Off!" I repeated. "Stop it. This is over."

Kirkland seemed to gradually return to himself. He let go of Art's collar—the detective's face looked like tenderized meat—and shifted his full attention to me. His own face was a stymied jumble of hate, sorrow, impotence.

"You haven't helped," he said. "You think you're helping. You're not."

Art squirmed free, and Martha rushed to cut the twine away from his wrists. Chunks of plaster and chipped paint fell from the ceiling—the rifle blast had blown a hole.

I kept my aim true on Kirkland. I didn't think I would have to fire, though. Because there was one last emotion in that jumble, laced through the hate and sorrow and impotence:

Relief.

"I don't pretend to know what's best," I said as Art produced a pair of handcuffs. "But I know what's right. This is right for the boys."

CHAPTER TWENTY

Jhonny and Calvin were found in decent shape, considering. Besides mild vitamin D deficiencies in both—despite the supplements Kent Kirkland had given them—their bodies were healthy. When the police took an ax to the fortified basement door, they hid together in a corner until the officers showed identification and explained they'd been rescued. Then they walked upstairs under their own power.

They would need substantial counseling. Jhonny had a minor panic attack at the police station on realizing he'd forgotten to take the crayon people he and Calvin had drawn, hundreds of them, all different colors and sizes and poses, each named and dated. He'd sobbed and needed Calvin brought in for comfort until a deputy returned from Kirkland's house with the stack of pages.

I knew all this from Art. He explained that the social workers didn't think the boys should meet us—me and Martha, the two people most responsible for their release. I agreed. They had enough to process, enough adjustments to make without having to find mental space for us.

The parents we did meet. The Witts were overcome with joy and gratitude. The father bear-hugged me until I asked for my breath back. They'd split up since Calvin's disappearance but vowed to cooperate and do better, to watch Calvin's diet, to keep track of him regardless of who had custody on any given day.

Art was skeptical. "You see her wrists, the sores? And his eyes?"

"They've got work to do," I said, having noticed the methamphetamine signs too. "But social services is going to keep testing them, right?"

He nodded. "Just the same, we're gonna run a black-and-white through the neighborhood every hour on the hour."

Becky Ramos brought her twins, who apparently hadn't recognized their older brother at first.

"I told them, 'It's Jon-Jon, Jon-Jon!'" Becky gushed, clutching Martha's arm. "But then he made his fishy-kissy face, and they knew. They knew."

She closed her eyes and broke into fresh peals of delight. Her Dollar General shift started at the top of the hour—she was wearing her black-and-yellow vest and name tag.

I asked what she'd heard from Jhonny's father.

"They're blaming me, of course," she said, speaking of the whole Venezuelan clan. "'We told you it wasn't us, we told you—it's all your fault.'"

Still, Becky seemed to be in a good place. She told us her parents, from whom she'd been estranged for years, had moved in from Utah to help with childcare. The twins let her talk to us with relatively little whining and sleeve tugging. Maybe they'd gotten long naps earlier. Jhonny was already asking about going back to school, though their caseworker was advising them to take things slow.

"I knew you'd bring good things," she said. "That day you came to visit, I just knew."

I smiled, remembering the New Age vibe of her place. "All I did was follow the clues. The one who made this happen, who started it, is Martha."

Standing beside me, Martha blushed and accepted Becky's further thanks with a ducked head and muted smile. One of the twins kept staring at her shoes, which featured felt carnations at the buckles.

"Do you like flowers?" Martha said, squatting to the girl's level.

She nodded brightly. "Piddy, piddy!"

Martha, recognizing "pretty" in toddler-speak, unclipped the flower and gave it to the girl.

Afterward, Martha and I said our farewells in the precinct parking lot. I hoped we would stay in touch—Martha had offered to babysit for me if I needed—but I knew it would be difficult. I had a backlog of McGill Investigators emails to answer, and Yancy Park was a healthy drive from Morristown. I would try. Next time Jennie did a Bunco Night, I'd see if they had space for one extra.

"How are things with Willard now?" I asked.

"Fine, we're fine," Martha said. "He did pay me back—he deposited half your fee into my account."

"Great."

She nodded with the air of someone trying to convince herself. "You know, not many husbands would've believed some guy down the street had two missing boys in his basement."

"No," I agreed. "It was out there."

We were briefly quiet. A uniformed officer walked out of the station with her eyes down on some document, found her squad car, and drove off. Through the windshield, she touched her visor toward us.

"Those neighbors who wrote letters," I said, changing the subject. "About Josh. Were you thinking of them when you saw Kirkland? When you started having suspicions?"

The subject had come up the day of Kirkland's arrest as we'd been tidying up, Martha reclipping the letters to the news article about her brother's death. I hadn't pressed her.

Now she looked heavenward. "No. I was thinking of two people who didn't have to write letters. Who lost the most, and never forgave themselves."

I stepped forward to embrace her, understanding she meant her mother and father.

"I'm sorry," I said into her quivering back. "I'm so sorry."

The next day, I drove down to We Will Rise! to thank Andre Wilcox for his cooperation. If he hadn't opened up his ledgers and shown me Jhonny's tutor list, I might've never connected the dots. Those boys might've still been drawing crayon companions in Kirkland's basement.

I brought Zach along.

"Hello, young man," Andre greeted him. "I understand you're no fan of the quadratic equation."

Zach brushed his bangs warily out of his eyes. I worried Andre had sunk our ship—I'd called in advance to ask about tutoring for Zach—but I guess he knew what he was doing because my usually obstinate teenager agreed with only minor grumping to the arrangement. I would drop him here twice a week for the rest of the semester.

"If it works out," Andre said, "if I can hook you up with a tutor you click with? Hey, we're in business. Happy trails otherwise."

Zach returned his frank look with a tight-lipped one of his own.

Watching them, I felt my heart flutter at how quickly, and irreversibly, this son of mine was growing up. Would this be the year Zach started taking his future seriously? The year he realized his time at home was running out and he ought to appreciate his family more?

A dreamy smile came to my lips. *A mother can hope, right?*

Next, Andre led us out to the lobby, where I supplied Zach's birth certificate and my driver's license. Andre had explained over the phone that they'd tightened their process after learning that "Knut Terwilliger"—whose routine background check had come back clean—was actually a ninety-four-year-old living in New Brunswick.

The receptionist, a middle-aged woman with hoop earrings, photocopied our documents.

I asked Andre, "What happened to Zeke?"

"He resigned. It was in the terms of his plea deal."

As Andre related how his former employee had phoned ahead to Kirkland after my initial visit and warned him his cover was blown, I gasped. *Of course!* I'd known somebody else must've been involved. Kirkland had found me at Martha's way too quickly that day.

"So he'll go to jail?" I said.

Andre made a squishy face. "Depends on the judge. Zeke's saying he didn't know about the basement. He thought Kirkland was getting the boys out to fosters who wanted them."

"You believe that?"

Andre inhaled, running a hand through gray stubble on his head. "Zeke went through the ringer with fosters, growing up. He and Kirkland talked about it. Turns out Kirkland wanted to be a foster himself, but social services turned him down. And he knew kids were getting sent willy-nilly to the Ferguson place. He and Zeke bonded over that. What crap it all was."

I wondered if that denial by social services had triggered Kirkland's mad kidnapping scheme. Putting myself in the caseworker's shoes, though, I could hardly blame them. A home tour from Kent Kirkland couldn't have been too reassuring.

I checked on Zach and found he'd drifted off to read a placard titled, *Anyone can be a father. It takes someone special to be a dad.*

I said, "People are complicated."

Andre grinned. "Amen to that."

We made it home from We Will Rise! by four o'clock, in time for me to prepare the Peruvian chicken and rice dish I'd bought ingredients for. I prepared the cilantro-broth slurry, then browned the chicken thighs.

I was flipping thighs when Jennie called.

"Bad time?" she asked. "I can call back later."

The kids were fighting sporadically upstairs, and Simba was kneading his front paws suspiciously into Zach's backpack—a material he had a history of peeing on.

"No worse than usual," I said. "What's up?"

"Patty and Meilin want to move Boody Burn to Thursday this week. Can you swing it?"

I checked my Catspirations calendar. "Sure. How's your day? Did Logan finally lose his tooth?"

"No, still dangling by a thread," Jennie said. "He won't let me touch it. Richard thinks we should get it tonight while he's asleep. Ooh, here's something! I decided on a name for the magazine."

"Nice." Using tongs, I spread the thighs evenly across the skillet. "You didn't go with *Morristown Moxie*, I hope?"

She laughed. "I settled on *Our Morristown*."

I waited for her to finish—*Our Morristown Gazette* or *Herald* or whatever. Apparently that was it.

Summoning cheer to my voice, I said, "Fantastic! I like it, it's simple. Homey."

"Thanks. My next step is to rustle up some advertisers. Have you thought any more about placing an ad for McGill Investigators?"

"A bit," I said. "My marketing budget is, you know, limited."

"Absolutely, no pressure," Jennie said. "Would your friend Durwood be interested? Doesn't he run a print ad in *Soldier of Fortune* for his injustice...thing?"

"I can ask. I do think, generally, he targets a more hard-scrabble-type clientele than the readers you're going for."

"Understood," Jennie said. A beeping started in the background. "Whoop, that's the timer. Gotta go pick up Olive Garden. See you Thursday, then? Bright and early?"

"Boody, boody, boody burn," I said, and clicked off.

In the skillet, my Peruvian chicken thighs were developing a nice color. I put down my phone and took out an onion and a cutting board.

Karen entered the kitchen. She boosted up on tiptoes, flashing a tight smile.

"D'you like?" she asked.

I was doing lengthwise cuts of the onion. "Like what?"

She twirled around. I felt my eyebrows move up my forehead.

"Your hair!" I said. "Where'd it go?"

In the next moment, Granny shuffled in holding the scissors high. "Onto the bathroom floor for your poor decrepit grandmother to pick up."

Karen rushed to apologize, but Granny waved her off with a denture-smacking frown.

The haircut was exactly what you might expect from a six-year-old's home job: jagged angles, a general rightward skew, and two stray rattails.

I said, "Honey, what was your, uh, thought process?"

"I was problem-solving!" she said.

I puffed my cheeks. *Walked right into that one.*

Granny put away the scissors and started poking around the stove. "What's shaking for dinner?" She pointed to the slurry. "That looks like cat sick."

I explained I was making Peruvian chicken from a recipe I'd found on a food blog.

Granny, who didn't trust a recipe unless it came from Julia Child, picked up the knife to give my onions an extra chop.

"What's wrong with baking a chicken?" she said. "Four hundred degrees, hour 'n' a half. Done. Who're you expecting, the Queen of Sheba?"

I pushed the chicken thighs to the edge of the pan and dumped in the onions. "I am expecting company, actually. Art Judd is going to join us for dinner."

She squinted, her mouth working wordlessly.

I prompted, "The detective."

"Oww, him? Mustache?"

I nodded. Her rheumy eyes turned thoughtful, and I

dreaded the next words out of her mouth. In the years she'd lived with us, my grandmother had called various romantic possibilities of mine "dolt," "dingbat," "Mr. Folgers," "louse" (Quaid Rafferty, multiple times), and "worthless as a sweet-smelling skunk."

A saucy expression came across her face. "Now that one might be worth impressing. I'll wear my gingham dress."

And off she went upstairs to change.

CHAPTER TWENTY-ONE

I'd had two dates with Art since the boys' rescue. Having eaten at his favorite place, we tried mine, a sandwich joint called Cafe Aioli. Then we went bowling. Both outings were fun and full of discovery—that Art had been a decent debater but a disastrous French horn player in high school, that our daughters, though a decade apart in age, had the same favorite movie: *The Parent Trap*.

Talking to Art with no case hanging over our heads felt wonderful, like jogging downhill after a long climb. He shared his dill pickle and confessed to murderous thoughts about Crystal's boyfriends. I kissed him after he picked up a 7-10 split, and gave him all the inside dirt about my outlandish adventures with Third Chance Enterprises.

After bowling, we went to Art's place and did more than kiss. In this, he was eager but gentle, funny during the inevitable hiccups, and every bit the outsize presence I'd sensed the day we'd met at the police station.

Still, I didn't know how things would go with the families involved. When I'd described him to the kids the other day, responding to Karen's "What is your new friend like?" question, Zach said he sounded like a cross between Paul Blart Mall Cop and a middle-school vice principal.

And what would Crystal think of me?

I built the sauce for my Peruvian chicken, adding the slurry and lowering to a simmer. Then I rallied the kids for a game of Scrabble while the flavors melded. Board games were my current go-to antidote for excessive phone time.

"Aw, I got a Z," Karen complained. "Z's are impossible."

"You *want* Z's," Zach said, rolling his eyes. "They're worth a ton of points. Duh."

Karen's lips pinched as she tried to think up a Z word. She glanced at my phone sitting on the coffee table but didn't ask to play SparklePopper.

She knew what my answer would be.

The doorbell rang as we were tallying up final scores. I quickly checked on dinner and my hair in the microwave reflection—full, only slightly lopsided—then answered.

Art Judd was wearing his badge. "You ready for this?"

He'd left his car running in the driveway. I zipped my jacket and joined him on the porch.

"Not especially," I said. "Did you decide about backup?"

Art nodded. "They'll be there."

We joined hands and walked to his car, which he keeps tidy for a man—I only had to move a few gas receipts to sit. Twenty minutes later, we pulled up to the Ferguson place.

A station wagon was parked in front, one wheel up on the curb. Art nosed in behind its rusted bumper.

"Backup's not here," he observed. "Should we wait or get this over with?"

I reached for my door handle. "Over with."

Art grabbed a document from the center console and slipped a hammer into his back pocket.

The yard was pocked with trash and bare dirt. Walking up a pebble path to the front door, an empty frame with the frayed remnants of a screen, I bent to retrieve a blowing plastic bag—then thought better of it. There was spaghetti with red sauce inside.

I hoped it was red sauce.

The house itself was a crumbling grande dame, three stories of dramatic turrets and spindles and sloughing-off shingles. Approaching the airy entrance, I kept close to Art. It smelled like a schmutzy kitchen sink with a slow drain.

Art knocked the frame. "Hello? Mr. and Mrs. Ferguson?"

A college-age kid with cutoff sleeves swaggered into view from a side room.

"They're indisposed," he said. "Who're you here for?"

"For them," Art said. "Can you get them, please?"

The kid took a sidelong look at Art's badge and disappeared up a staircase.

I ventured a few steps inside, Art following cautiously. The chaos made me want to drive a plow through the place. Crumpled papers and unopened mail covered a coffee table (two tables?), waterfalling to the ground. The carpet squished on one stride and partially gave out on the next as though my shoe had found a sinkhole.

The only tidy thing about the place was a floor-to-ceiling bookcase whose titles were arranged short to tall, spines neat, edges aligned.

Kent Kirkland's words came back to me. *Books deserve to be free.*

Vincent and Maeve Ferguson emerged in sweatpants and T-shirts, his featuring a Che Guevara silhouette.

"Warrant?" Maeve said.

Her aggressive question reminded me instantly of her son. The severe jawline was the same too.

"Don't need it today," Art said, showing his document. "We're here to condemn this dwelling. You have twenty-four hours to vacate the premises."

Vincent opened his mouth to speak, but Maeve cut him off. "That's outrageous."

"You were warned multiple times."

"No, we weren't."

Art produced a second paper from his breast pocket. "Officer Bruce paid a visit February four. March sixteen, Officer Menendez came by—"

"So what?" Maeve gripped her husband's hand defiantly. "You can't do this without proper notice."

Art gestured to the paper sea behind us. "I'm thinking we could find some if we looked."

Vincent spoke up in an affected highbrow tone, "Our associates at city hall will be disheartened to hear of this blind-side assault."

I knew I should've left official business to Art, but I couldn't help jumping in.

"Funny thing about associates," I said. "They don't like being *associated* with kidnapping and high-profile cases of neglect."

The aging grifters acted confused, but I saw in their stiffened necks: they knew exactly what I was talking about.

"Do you even care?" I asked. "What became of your son, what you did to him?"

Maeve faltered, then seemed to decide pretending was pointless.

"He betrayed me—he turned on us," she said. "I'm not responsible. I put a roof over his head. I gave him meals when he needed 'em."

Her eyes and mouth trembled in another echo of her son. I looked past her to the squalor. There was a card game going in the kitchen, a half dozen kids ranging from five to fifteen, passing around Doritos and a two-liter of soda.

"A roof over his head and meals when he needed them," I repeated.

Maeve stewed over this. Vincent ran a hand through her lank gray hair, then rested it on her shoulder. Finally, she turned to Art.

"The news said they're holding him in some psych ward," she said. "Evaluating him before they press charges?"

"Trenton Psychiatric," Art confirmed.

The woman mastered herself. "How much time you think he...would you figure they..."

Her eyes kept finding the tattered carpet. She didn't seem capable of saying the word "jail."

Art said, "They'll get him on two counts first-degree kidnapping. Twenty-five years to life, times two."

Maeve kept a stoic expression, but her legs shifted as if to save her from stumbling or fainting.

There was more to the story, I knew. Art had clued me in. The attorney general's office had pushed for harsh treatment during the initial maelstrom of media coverage. "Yancy Park Neat Freak Who Imprisoned Missing Boys: 'Time With Me Was the Best of Their Lives!'" But the spotlight had quickly passed. A high-profile defense attorney had intervened and begun negotiating on Kirkland's behalf.

Would Art provide any of his inside information now? Maeve Ferguson certainly didn't deserve it.

After a pregnant moment, though, he continued, "Kent won't do twenty-five. New Jersey has what's called 'affirmative defense.' If you can prove you thought your action was necessary to prevent 'imminent danger to the victim,' it's mitigating. They can argue insanity too."

Art exhaled. "He's probably looking at ten years. Seven or eight with parole."

Maeve scowled in response, but I could tell she was covering her emotions. One hand squeezed the waist of her sweatpants.

Vincent croaked, "Sounds f-fair."

We all stood around considering this, air hitting our backs through the missing front door.

Art took out his hammer and looked for a place to nail up the condemnation document. "Can you communicate to all these folks? Or should I get my bullhorn?"

The Fergusons said they would handle the evacuation. Art left behind a stack of cards with information for juvenile services and a nearby homeless shelter.

As we walked back to the car, Art's hand sought mine. In the distance below, I could just make out Kent Kirkland's high privacy fence. It looked small and pointless from here, and started me thinking about boundaries. How important they were for children and neighbors. How sometimes they were hard and other times soft, how religiously you had to tend them. How difficult they were to get right.

"Those kids of yours," Art said. "I'm nervous."

I chuckled. "You don't look nervous."

He fixed the tuck of his shirt and loosened his tie. "It's been a while since I talked to a six-year-old. And I don't know the first thing about skateboarding."

Now we were sitting in his car, talking across the center console. "I'll bet you figure it out."

He smiled, and we leaned together to kiss. His mouth felt soft and easy, a place you'd like to stay forever. My hand found his pants below. The polyester felt scratchy and pleasant on my skin.

When our kiss broke, Art's gaze landed on his badge, which he'd place on the dashboard. He put his key in the ignition.

"I've disappointed people before," he said. "I haven't meant to."

I slid my hand down to his knee, and waited on his eyes to come back.

"We'll be disappointed together," I said. "Or maybe we won't."

Keep reading for a sneak peek at book four
in the Third Chance Enterprises saga,
featuring Quaid Rafferty:

ASTROPLANE

ASTROPLANE

Sneak Peek

When Zhao Ng aimed his gyrotron in the general direction of the facility, its needle twitched. He couldn't know how much of the nuclear material the instrument had swept. If any. It was three a.m., and the sky was moonless—the reason his commanders had chosen tonight for the mission.

Zhao lay on his stomach in the hillside berm, beside the trunk of an ancient beech tree. He'd hiked seven kilometers from the helicopter drop, and now smelled his own body together with mud and forest rot.

Still, his lungs felt new here, away from fetid Beijing. His muscles were alive with the promise of action.

He shifted the mouth of the gyrotron. Zhao had just a thumb and forefinger for a left hand—the rest he'd lost defending the Republic's interests in the Arctic Circle—so he twisted with his right. The instrument hummed like a cicada.

He squinted into the black expanse. One pass of the gyrotron produced another needle twitch. For the second, he moved its mouth painstakingly, millimeter by millimeter.

Halfway across the facility's face, the needle sprang to the far right of its gauge.

Nuclear. A reading of that amplitude left no doubt.

He packed the gyroscope back into its case, careful of the wires, and buried it in the hillside earth. Next, he slipped crampons over his boots and started down the grade, anchoring himself by beech trunks where possible.

He kept his center of gravity near the ground. He silenced his comm. He broke few twigs. The hillside was unlikely to be under surveillance, but Zhao would leave nothing to chance.

The descent took an hour.

At last, he reached the base of the hill. He took night-vision goggles from his pack and, maintaining cover, swung the goggles along a barbed-wire fence line. Each corner of the perimeter was manned by a guard.

The distance from his current position to the fence line was forty-three meters. The entire way was barren. Not a utility outpost, nor tree, nor even much grass. The two nearest guards had unfettered field of vision.

His commanders had considered tunnels, but the time required to dig that far was prohibitive.

Zhao himself had suggested being dropped directly into the facility, but his longtime mission pilot—the Austrian, Horst—had scoffed at the idea.

So, the tripod and rifle.

Zhao removed his crampons and, scouting a flat patch of dirt, popped stiff the legs of his tripod. He confirmed clean line of sight to the first guards.

The northeast corner was closest, but the southeast

provided the easiest shot. The fence surrounding that guard station was lower.

Zhao dropped to one knee and pressed his forehead into the weapon's eyecup. He took aim. With his deformed left hand, he tuned the scope until he could see the horizontal stripes of his target's flag patch.

He fired. His target dropped out of the night.

Zhao had used a silencer, but the shot's echo still threatened to reveal his position.

He moved the muzzle, swiftly but without hurry, onto the northeast corner. This guard had begun scurrying at the noise. Zhao aimed through diamond-mesh fence. The guard's head whipped south, then back toward the hillside, directly at Zhao.

Zhao fired. The blast knocked the guard off his feet, toppling his duty chair.

Now Zhao did hurry. The Loud Phase had begun: he had precisely seven minutes until extraction.

He sprinted over the forty-three-meter no-man's-land. Urging out over his knees, pain pricking his left foot, right hip, pelvic bone—parts the Ministry of State Security had repaired over the years with pins or shark cartilage.

The guards from the facility's western corners had long runs themselves to intercept Zhao. And they wouldn't realize they were racing.

Zhao reached the vehicle gate, the only non-electrified portion of the fence, and dove to a prone position.

He'd abandoned his tripod, and there was no time to assemble it anyway. He pulled a shortgun from his bag. He trained its nightscope on the spot where the third guard should appear, the leftmost edge of the building.

The moment the man turned the corner, Zhao stopped him.

Zhao hadn't used a silencer, there being no point. The gun's report boomed about the valley.

How is the fourth guard reacting?

This would be the most challenging kill, Zhao knew. If the final guard reached for his walkie-talkie or phone, Zhao could soon face a swarm. Seven minutes might be enough to beat the swarm.

Or it might not.

If the guard was brave and rushed directly to the disturbance, Zhao would drop him like the first three.

Otherwise, Zhao might be forced into a protracted cat-and-mouse through the facility. Listening at doors. Using smokers and the infrared detector.

No—in seven minutes, he couldn't. Zhao would have no choice but to proceed directly with the mission objective. He would be forced to do his intricate work while keeping one eye out for the guard. Not an ideal scenario.

He hoped for the man's bravery.

Zhao felt every pebble against his chest and groin. He watched the edge of the building. Night breeze whistled across a sliver of exposed skin on his calf.

He waited five seconds.

Ten.

Just as Zhao decided he could wait no longer, a white-green mass appeared in his scope. The mass was hunched over and rounded the corner warily. A man.

A brave man.

Zhao fired into the center of the mass. He wasted no time confirming the result, scrambling up an asphalt drive to a loading bay.

He used bolt cutters to snap a chain securing the handle of an accordion roll-up grate. Then he yanked the grate open.

Tick-tick-tick-tick-tick...wham!

One step inside, motion-detector lights blared alive—stark, from bulbs as big as bears. The hangar was cavernous, a two-hundred-foot ceiling girded by a spiderweb of steel. The greatest part of the space was occupied by the thing itself.

Astroplane.

Zhao staggered at the size of the craft. (And Zhao was no stranger to gargantuan structures, having battled Mongolian separatists on the spillway of the Three Gorges Dam.) Mountains of scaffolding surrounded its sides, which bowed gently like a whale's—only instead of blubber, Zhao knew, they contained heat-reflecting panels to protect against the rigors of reentry.

Planes like the X-15 and SpaceShipOne had flirted with outer space, nearly exiting Earth's atmosphere using external rockets or a second craft. Astroplane would be the first to enter and maintain orbit all on her own.

A unicorn.

Zhao located the main rocket engine and dashed up the nearest scaffolding, taking the switchbacking steps three per stride. His pack weighed him down. His legs burned. The scaffolding rocked with his boots' force. Twice, he nearly fell.

Up close, Astroplane seemed cold and coiled. Restless. Zhao couldn't have said why, but he felt the craft wanted to cast off her braces and overwraps and be on with it.

She wanted to fly.

"*Soon,*" Zhao said aloud, arriving at the engine.

He peered into the maw of a bell-shaped nozzle. The Ministry believed the thermonuclear engine was ready to fly as is, but Zhao noticed the casing was off its turbopump.

Are they repairing it? Has some design flaw been discovered?

Zhao only troubled over the issue a moment. It was a problem for the engineers back in Beijing.

He scaled the engine, using the textures of the inner nozzle to gain purchase. The sides of Astroplane had no texture, and so he pulled crampons back over his boots in order to climb the rest of the way. His hands' grip—those seven good fingers —was precarious. He paused often to regroup, even as the mission clock was ticking down loudly in his head.

Finally, Zhao stood atop the craft. It felt like he was surfing a continent.

He hinged his neck to look straight up into the steel girders. They were another thirty or forty feet higher.

He found rope and a scaffolding hook in his pack. Bending at the knees for power, he flung the hook high into the air.

It clattered back to him on the first and second tries. On the third, the hook caught a crossbeam. It had stuck in such a place that the rope dangled several feet away from Astroplane.

Zhao leaned out, his second foot losing contact, and grabbed it.

A gunshot rent the air.

Zhao felt the bullet nick his pant leg. His eyes darted to the hangar floor. Quickly, he identified the source—that fourth guard sitting in a heap, badly damaged from Zhao's first shot.

Zhao hustled his rope end to the center of Astroplane's

roof, away from the guard's line of sight. He wasn't about to surrender the rope and go leaning into the void again.

He secured the rope end beneath three heavy blocks of C-4, retrieved his shortgun, and stomach-crawled back to the side of the craft.

He peeked over the precipice of Astroplane.

The wounded guard lay near the entrance to the loading bay. Though it was a great distance, Zhao saw him jerking his weapon side to side, up and down, desperate to locate the intruder.

No doubt he would have used his walkie-talkie. Zhao needed to hurry.

He centered the guard in his crosshairs and finished the kill.

Alone in the hangar, Zhao resumed his work. He tied the bricks of C4 to the rope using a bowline knot, affixed a sufficient length of det cord, and pulleyed the explosives hand over hand until they'd reached the crossbeam anchoring the hook.

The det cord lilted through the vast hangar: a brittle, lethal tail.

Zhao grabbed the det cord's end and descended the scaffolding, careful not to tangle it through the crisscrossing supports. Twice, the det cord snapped taut on him and he had to add another length.

Hopping off the lowest platform to the hangar floor, he stared up into Astroplane's belly—where one day suitcases might be stowed for the thirty-minute hop from Mumbai to Mexico City.

He activated his chemical lighter and held its flame to the det cord. The cord flashed blue and orange, a snake of fire rushing instantly skyward, up the side of Astroplane, through the hangar's upper reaches to its steel girding.

GooooOOOOMMM!

The roof sundered. Chunks of metal and steel fell all around Zhao, banging the scaffolding, shattering windows. Zhao crouched in the hollow created by Astroplane's body, which bore the brunt of the debris.

The top and much of the craft's sides were destroyed. Multiple alarms were bleating. Dust clogged Zhao's nose and stung his eyes. A fire on the hangar's near side smelled tangy and putrid. He hoped it wasn't rocket fuel.

In the middle of all this destruction, Zhao focused. He donned his welding goggles and blowtorch. He identified a section of scaffolding that remained passable and climbed it.

Reaching the engine, he began shearing it away from Astroplane. The junction with the passenger cabin was thick. He had to keep his torch's flame steady several seconds before moving along.

The heat on Zhao's face was terrific. Sweat poured off his brow, dripping to the concrete far below.

He was perhaps two-thirds of the way through the joint when a helicopter's roar filled the air.

Horst.

Zhao wouldn't waste time checking, but he knew the mission clock was approaching 7:00.

He moved his blowtorch faster now, not waiting to observe clear separation between Astroplane's engine and its cabin.

Dimly, Zhao was aware of his hair whipping in the rotor wash. He kept cutting. The flame was quite close to the joint and sheltered by Zhao's body—even so, it flickered in the wind.

Zhao closed his mind to this, to everything.

When he'd severed or weakened as much steel as he figured was needed, he looked up.

On cue, precisely as they'd practiced it off the coast of Xiamen, four cables descended from the helicopter. Zhao grabbed their hooked ends and attached each stoutly to the jet's nozzle and turbopumps.

He tugged to be sure of their attachment, then he flashed thumbs-up to Horst. Through the window, his partner of fourteen years returned the signal.

Zhao jumped onto the engine. He blazed a last line along the section of steel he'd only weakened, then threw the blowtorch away.

In another moment, the helicopter thrust up. The remaining junction gave the briefest whine of protest, then snapped apart.

The engine jerked higher. Zhao held on for his life, one hand in the nozzle and the other around a cable. The bulky engine swayed and rolled as it was lifted out of the hangar.

Clearing the top of the facility, Zhao removed a detonator from his backpack and then hurled the pack back down at Astroplane.

Horst began winching him in. The engine's bucking was more violent than it had been at Xiamen, as if the engine were fighting off its thieves.

Zhao gripped the detonator. Range was an issue. These cheap devices used radio frequencies rated to two hundred meters, but Horst had said it would be "advisable" to wait until they'd cleared the hangar by two hundred fifty.

Helicopters and pressure waves did not mix.

The bucking continued. The wind only worsened as they rose above the tree line. Zhao watched the hangar and mentally gauged their altitude, counting in silence, multiplying, making odds...

Beijing would be enraged if he didn't destroy the remainder of the plane. With the thermonuclear engine in hand and the existing Astroplane destroyed, Chinese engineers would beat the foreigners to a flight-ready vessel. They didn't have workers' rights and a two-chambered legislature to muddle through. Most technical challenges had already been overcome, and the last questions should be answered easily by the mechanism Zhao was riding atop now.

If Astroplane was not destroyed, but only damaged?

The future became less clear. It would depend how the twin engine on the craft's opposite side fared, whether it could be fixed. How quickly the repairs could be done.

China might lose.

With ten meters of cable still separating Zhao from the helicopter, he pressed the detonator button.

The world below became a fireball. Zhao and the stolen engine were blasted higher, swinging alongside the cockpit, knocking its glass side. Zhao saw Horst fighting the stick, holding it two-handed in place, his face twisted with effort.

Zhao dug his fingers deeper into the nozzle's interior, improving his grip. He pressed his face to the steel. The helicopter dipped erratically, and he feared being dragged through the canopy of beech trees, but Horst recovered their ascent.

The winch kept winding Zhao in. Smells of gas and incinerated building materials overwhelmed the river valley's sweet notes.

It was quiet now, at least.

As they climbed the night sky, Zhao considered the hangar and its surrounding countryside. The facility resembled the shoebox of a child who collects scarred, blackened rocks.

Could Astroplane have survived?

Surely not.

Zhao pulled himself closer using a landing skid, and climbed inside the cabin by the escape hatch.

Horst swiveled in the pilot's chair. His glass eye was gray and opaque as ever, but his good one sparkled.

In Mandarin, he said, "You forgot what two hundred fifty meters looks like?"

Zhao growled off the quip, but he was grinning. He found the helicopter's comm and radioed Beijing the job was done.

ASTROPLANE

Sneak Peek

Six prairie fires into his Tuesday afternoon, Quaid Rafferty still hadn't beaten the itch. Every article in every magazine in the cabana bored him. The water was too still. The sky too blue. He'd slept with each of the three women suntanning here at the Bacchus Pool of Caesars Palace, two of them merely attractive and one of them homely—a divorcee from Kansas City with a gift of gab to rival Quaid's—and now he wanted...

What?

From the next cabana: "This ceviche is garbage. *Blech*—did anyone even clean the halibut?"

Quaid glanced through a slit in the cabana's canvas. A hotel guest he'd heard variously called "Bammer" and "Bam-Bam" was berating a server. Words and puffs of cigar smoke took turns blasting forth from Bammer's puffy lips.

The young server worried her hands at her waist. "The cooks try to, thoroughly. But I'll have a fresh batch made at once."

She scurried off without being thanked, Bammer still

chewing. Apparently the ceviche wasn't bad enough to stop eating—just to bitch about.

As the man sat back, his eyes roamed the cabana and found Quaid's.

Quaid said, "You got fish poop on your collar."

Bammer looked down at his shirt, aghast, compressing his second and third chins. "What? Where?"

"Other side." Quaid nodded to his far collar. "Little black string. See it?"

The man frantically inspected the fabric, stretching it away from his chest, knocking over a frozen drink.

"I don't see nothing. That's a pattern—you talking about my pattern?"

Quaid made a face. "I think it's fish poop."

Bammer pulled his collar this way and that. "It's a pattern. It's a chambray shirt, it's not white."

"Yep," Quaid said. "It's not white."

Bammer fretted over his shirt another minute, spilling his cigar ashes, spoiling his towel in the slushy red remnants of his drink.

"Hey," he said, "you're screwing with me."

Quaid smirked and picked up the next journal on his reading stack, a double issue of *Audubon* devoted to climate change.

Eyes on the first article, he said, "Next time, shut up and eat what she brings you."

He let a trace of menace into his tone. Bammer left it alone—whether because he knew of Quaid's Third Chance Enterprises resume or was just spineless, no telling.

When the new ceviche arrived, Bammer took it to the hot tub.

Quaid tried focusing on methane chemistry. He was

between jobs at the moment and cruising for work. Generally clients sought Quaid out, but he found it profitable to keep abreast of hot-button geopolitical issues. He believed the environmental realm was ripe for intrigue.

Over the top of his magazine, Quaid saw the server approaching.

"Perfect timing, I'm just now ready for you." Downing the last third of his drink, he handed her the empty along with a twenty-dollar tip. "You can't expect much from your day until you've had lucky number seven."

The woman rolled her eyes conspiratorially. He'd noticed her waiting for orders at the bar station, sipping from a clear glass with relish—the sort of relish no drinker takes in water.

She brought a check folio out from behind her back. "Mr. Rafferty, I-I'm afraid your card was declined."

Quaid quirked his mouth. "No kidding? Must be some blip with the bank."

"Of course," she said. "Perhaps you have another card I can run?"

He patted around his trunks, then underneath his lounger, and finally found his American Express Gold in the breast pocket of his sport coat—folded neatly over a bamboo table.

The server ferried it and the empty glass away.

Quaid was dismayed. He'd figured the Visa would hold up at least another month. Clearly he'd overshot his summer budget—either for food, alcohol, or philanthropic expenditures. Likely all three.

How big a check did I cut Human Rights Watch?

They'd had a big push going to oppose the speech crackdown in Guinea, and Quaid—who'd been a longtime champion of progressive causes as Massachusetts governor before being brought low by bogus solicitation charges—had given generously.

He *should* be flush with cash. It hadn't been even a full year since they'd reversed worldwide anarchy. American Dynamics had paid out handsomely for that job, and in the wake of the windfall, Quaid supposed his command of incoming credits vis-à-vis outgoing debits must've waned.

Whoops.

Possibly he shouldn't have flown to Ibiza with the mayor of New York City. Or done that two-month side-hustle for Greenpeace pro bono. The jet pack alone, for sneaking into Dr. Zhorrgum's condor enclosure, had cost two hundred grand.

The server returned with a pained expression.

"I do apologize," she said, holding the credit card between them. "But this one was also declined."

Quaid shrugged, holding out his hand to take it back.

She said, "They—er, the representative instructed me to shred the card. Again, I apologize."

"Not at all." He raised his hands in a sort of *ah, what's it to me?* flourish. "It's for the best. The APR on that card was downright usurious."

The woman nodded her understanding but stayed where she stood, awaiting a valid method of payment.

Quaid whistled and stretched a hand high overhead, bringing it down through his wavy blond hair.

Well? He could sleep with her. He could call Durwood Oak Jones, his Third Chance partner, and ask for a loan—though the idea of wheedling the plainspoken West Virginian over the phone made Quaid's head hurt.

He could ask a favor of one of the myriad Nevada officials he knew from his gubernatorial days. Quaid had stumped for the current attorney general—doubtless the man could score him some breathing room with Caesars.

Sleeping with the server would be easiest, and most fun. He was just gazing into those honey-green eyes and selecting the perfect word to describe them when he caught sight of Bammer emerging from the hot tub.

"You know what? I forgot." Quaid released the woman's hand, which he'd taken. "My generous neighbor and I decided to alternate tabs. Since he's always over here"— Quaid mimed a chug, head tipped back—"we agreed he'd go ahead and pay for day one."

She straightened up, possibly remembering the non-generosity of Bammer's ceviche fit. "You're...quite sure?"

Quaid gathered his *Audubon* and sport coat off the bamboo table. "You bet." He stood. "I think I'll go chase the sun. All of a sudden, I'm in full shade here. Can you bring my next round over to the swim-up blackjack tables? Better make it a double too. Nothing's worse for my luck than gambling sober."

He picked his way over hot Roman tiles to Temple Pool, the next pool over. He watched hotel guests tanning, reading romance novels, flirting, minding kids, getting drunk, minding kids *and* getting drunk...

Halfway to his favored swim-up blackjack dealer, a voice stopped him.

"Mr. Rafferty."

For a moment, he figured it would be Bammer. Upon further reflection, though, he realized the voice was too deep. Too dignified.

"I've heard," the voice said, "that you are a man who makes things happen."